THE CROOKED MAN

The life and crimes of Thomas Bates are fated to spiral with a horrid inevitability from petty thievery to murder. There's Grace Pickering, whose life he saves and who rewards him with a passionate affection he attempts to avoid — until he learns about her savings account, marrying her only to plunder it and leave her. His next victim, a man, he is forced to kill. Eventually he returns to Grace when she inherits wealth, and thereafter, her days seem numbered . . . but how long can Bates's depredations continue unchecked?

Books by Shelley Smith
in the Linford Mystery Library:

THE LORD HAVE MERCY
COME AND BE KILLED
THIS IS THE HOUSE
THE CELLAR AT NO. 5
BACKGROUND FOR MURDER
DEATH STALKS A LADY
STING OF DEATH
THE MISSING SCHOOLGIRL

Pi
You c
or by us
phone
card a
You

SPECIAL MESSAGE TO READERS

THE ULVERSCROFT FOUNDATION
(registered UK charity number 264873)
was established in 1972 to provide funds for
research, diagnosis and treatment of eye diseases.
Examples of major projects funded by
the Ulverscroft Foundation are:-

- The Children's Eye Unit at Moorfields Eye Hospital, London
- The Ulverscroft Children's Eye Unit at Great Ormond Street Hospital for Sick Children
- Funding research into eye diseases and treatment at the Department of Ophthalmology, University of Leicester
- The Ulverscroft Vision Research Group, Institute of Child Health
- Twin operating theatres at the Western Ophthalmic Hospital, London
- The Chair of Ophthalmology at the Royal Australian College of Ophthalmologists

You can help further the work of the Foundation
by making a donation or leaving a legacy.
Every contribution is gratefully received. If you
would like to help support the Foundation or
require further information, please contact:

THE ULVERSCROFT FOUNDATION
The Green, Bradgate Road, Anstey
Leicester LE7 7FU, England
Tel: (0116) 236 4325
website: www.foundation.ulverscroft.com

SHELLEY SMITH

THE
CROOKED
MAN

Complete and Unabridged

LINFORD
Leicester

First published in Great Britain

First Linford Edition
published 2019

*A catalogue record for this book is available
from the British Library.*

ISBN 978–1–4448–4080–3

Published by
F. A. Thorpe (Publishing)
Anstey, Leicestershire

Set by Words & Graphics Ltd.
Anstey, Leicestershire
Printed and bound in Great Britain by
T. J. International Ltd., Padstow, Cornwall

This book is printed on acid-free paper

1

Ma Would Turn in Her Grave

You could hear him coming the length of the empty blazing street. The sharp echo of wood on pavement, a measured rapping as sinister as Blind Pew's and then the gruesome shuffle of a dragging foot.

Slung between crutches with his shoulders hunched to his ears, he resembled, as he hopped along in his khaki drabs, some huge nondescript bird. And his eyes continually glanced up sideways at the windows from his down-bent face, the way birds look. Something birdlike too, about the frail-boned skull with its eyes set in a little crooked and oddly wide apart: eyes the color of anthracite.

Not a soul alive! He'd have to swing the length of the street; and his armpits were on fire from the chafing crutches, the dangling leg so awkwardly bent at the knee already giving him hell. The sweat

1

— no kidding! — was pricking out on his skin.

A woman appeared at the top of the road. He did not raise his head to look at her, but the little rapid clatter of her heels was as neat as a thrush breaking a snail on a path. The nearer she came, the slower he advanced. Till as she drew level, he collapsed sideways against a low brick wall and slid not ungracefully down at her feet. A crutch rattled between her heels.

To step over it and walk on was not a thing many people would or could do. This woman stopped, bent down, distressed, to utter the foolish queries that spring to the lips at such a time.

He did not speak. His eyes were closed. In the shadow of his Anzac hat, his face glistened pallidly; beads of water clustered at his temples, ran down his hollowed cheeks.

'Here, Tommy,' she said desperately, 'have you fainted?'

His lids slipped back into his head like a doll's; his eyes stared blank into hers.

'I'll be okay,' he croaked in a weary sort of whisper. 'If I had somewhere I could rest for a minute or two ... done up ... done in,' he muttered in a rank but not unpleasant cockney.

To refuse help to a sick man, a cripple, a soldier, is not a thing many people would or could do. With her shrewd blue eyes she read him off from left to right, and summed him up as harmless enough. The collapsed limbs, the white exhaustion, eyes sunken behind their cheekbones, the jaw razor sharp, mouth a grim line rendered total pathos.

Her house was only a couple of doors away. With her help he clambered along, sank at last into a womb-deep armchair in her cool north-facing lounge. His head rolled back. The crutches sprawled. She took off his hat and smoothed back the dark feathers that fitted so neatly over his skull, very soft and agreeable to the touch. The feel of it made her hand, then her heart, then her mind more tender. It gave her a little shock to see his dead dark eyes staring at her.

'I'll get you a drop of brandy,' she said quickly.

'Don't,' he said, putting out a hand. 'I

never touch it. Fair dinkum!'

'This is medicine; not booze.'

'Truly. I'd much rather have a cuppa tea, if it's not a liberty.' He gave her a crooked smile.

'I might have known an old digger would sooner have tea than a 'pot',' she laughed.

A second's apprehension twitched his impassive face.

'Don't tell me you're Aussie, too?' he hazarded.

'Not me, no. But I met a lot of your cobbers when I ran a mobile canteen in the war, and I know what they like all right.'

She had a fine lot of teeth in her smile. He flinched from them inwardly. While she went to 'pop the kettle on,' he gazed about him alertly, analyzing the room: mahogany furniture, the heavy good sort of stuff that was inherited; bits of pewter about; sweet peas in a silver bowl; some nice-looking odds and ends in a cabinet, Dresden figures and that, and what they call cloisonné boxes; little Jap ivories on the table by the window, too; nice stuff.

He sighed and stretched out his good leg.

'Cigarette?' She stood before him shaking them gently in a silver box.

He shook his head.

'No, thanks. I don't smoke.'

'You don't smoke; you don't drink: you're too good to be true! No wonder you pass out in the street.'

'It's just that I'm weak still; only just been discharged. It's the crutches, that's my trouble. Not used to 'em yet, and they rub shocking: raw as beef under my arms.' He put a handkerchief delicately as a maiden to his upper lip.

'Perhaps you won't need them much longer.'

'They tell me I won't ever walk again,' he said casually. 'Bit a shrapnel in the knee. Lucky to save my leg, so they told me; though I'm blowed if I know what use it is.' He shrugged sardonically to show he wasn't grizzling.

'Oh God,' she sighed, 'what a war!' And went to make tea.

He listened intently to the sound of her footsteps in the kitchen and the chinking of china, a menacing look on his unselfconscious face. He stood up and with a grin of pure anguish straightened his gammy leg from its agonizing cramp. A step this way, a step that — the room was not large, though crowded with effects. In the gloom of the mirror he caught sight of his head turning alertly like a deer in the forest. Beneath the faked sweat the real sweat sprang.

(The faked sweat lent a touch of pathos to his natural pallor and made his rather wooden impassivity seem gallant. Alas for him, he could not act, he could not even feel himself into a part he had played as many times as this one, and he was obliged to convey the impressions he wanted to make by numerous little faked touches applied outwardly. In the same way he passed off the cockney tinge in his voice by passing as an Australian. There were other advantages to it as well, he found; to be colonial had all the romance of being foreign without any suspicious foreignness; also one was supposed to be slightly more gullible than a native, and that was an advantage too.)

She was back with the tea things

quicker than you'd think, seating herself unnervingly between him and the door. That faintly rattled him and to keep her attention quietly on himself he was obliged to talk rather more than he cared to, volunteering the information about himself that he preferred to have pried out of him by questions. The less said the better, he always thought, and was instinctively laconic even when, as now, he wished to appear confiding.

Attending to the tea rite, she yet found her eye wandering, returning to the little cabinet, disturbed by an abstract of shadow that made an unusual pattern: yet the clipped voice successfully prevented it becoming a question in her mind.

' . . . so that by the time I was twenty-seven I had over six thousand head of sheep,' the clipped voice was saying.

'Where was this?' she asked, hurrying to catch up.

'My station? Two hundred miles north of Brisbane. That's Queensland. You c'n ride for miles there without seeing another soul. You'd think you were in Paradise.'

7

'Paradise!' She gazed at him in amusement, struck by this fancy, her attention at last distracted from the dense patch of shadow on the cabinet, and asked, 'So your idea of Paradise has no other people in it? Adam without Eve, eh?'

He gave her a cheeky eye.

'Paradise *with* Eve didn't last long, by all accounts, did it?' he jested.

But at her words he had been pierced by the sharpness of his sudden desire for the Paradise of a world unpeopled, all to himself. It had never occurred to him to imagine for himself a Heaven other than in the terms taught him in the Institution: a Heaven of harps cascading eternal psalms against a boredom of infinite blue, with seas of jasper and chalcedony below, hard and slippery as glass; and everywhere, as far as the eye could see, people, an endless multitude of people, clothed in white, praising everlastingly, with himself — if he was there at all — nothing but a meaningless dot among so many. But the whole world to oneself! That was ecstasy! The mere conception caused the soul to expand with delight. The pressure of deceit and envy that distorted so cruelly one's personality would no longer exist, and instead one would know the pure bliss of being oneself, master of the solitudes.

'Pardon?' he said, looking quite dazed.

'I said, what made you leave this ranch of yours, or whatever you call this Paradise, then?'

'Oh, that! They talked me into coming over to win the war for them,' he said dryly. 'Fancied myself as some sort of hero, I reckon. So I put a chap in to manage my station and went down to Sydney.' He gave his crooked smile: 'And in two years' time I was ruined. There's gratitude for you!'

'How d'you mean, ruined?' she asked uneasily.

He drained his cup and put it down carefully.

'Like this. My own fault, maybe you'll say. But it turned out this chap I put in knew as much about sheep-farming as a deep-sea fisherman. The first year he came a mucker over the price, the second year he lost more than half the herd with sheep rot. Then he chucked in his hand. What could I do, half the world away, in the middle of a war? They put the place up for auction; only by that time there wasn't anything left worth auctioning. The sale just about covered the expenses. I never saw any of it, I know that.'

'What a rotten shame,' she said. 'I do call that rotten.'

'What they call the fortunes of war.' He shrugged gallantly.

'I suppose so. And some, after all, fared worse.'

'Oh, I'm not complaining,' he said wryly. 'I've still got my brains and one good leg.'

She said encouragingly, 'You'll go back and start again, and build it up bigger than before.'

'Not me. I'm out, far as that's concerned. It was a good life while it lasted, but it's no living for a cripple. I couldn't even sit a horse now, me that used to be in the saddle eight or ten hours a day!'

'I'm sorry. I really am sorry,' she

sighed, looking away from him, letting her eye wander disconsolately, for who would not be depressed by these endless tragedies that left one feeling helpless, guilty, discomforted?

'Oh, I'll make a living somehow,' he said cheerfully. 'I mustn't trouble you with my troubles.' He stood up, tucking his crutches under his arms, watching her nervously hunting for a cigarette. He began his awkward farewells. But she was not strictly attending, looking about her, bewildered, for the silver cigarette box that was no longer on the little table where she had left it beside the netsukes.

She noticed with a little shock of surprise that the old man with the dragon on his back was missing from among the netsukes and the woman washing her feet.

A flush burst into her face.

And, glancing now at the cabinet in intuitive comprehension, she saw clearly that the puzzling shadow was occasioned by a blank space (it was either the miniature of Napoleon or the Queen Anne patchbox, or both). She fumed with anger at this dirty trick. Nipping between the soldier and the door, she barred his way, confronting him boldly.

'Come on!' she said harshly. 'Hand them over! Hurry up! I'll give you just thirty seconds, m'lad, before I send for the police.'

He gave her a quick look, himself expressionless, and then unbuttoned his tunic and slowly took out the little glittering objects that a magpie might have stowed away.

'*You dirty swine!*' she exclaimed, cut to the quick to see her worst suspicions come true. 'Coming in here, spinning me the tale, and drinking my tea! You ought to be horsewhipped! I only wish my husband was home. He'd give you the hiding you deserve.' But her husband had been dead for six years, alas.

'Sorry,' he said.

Her fury mounted at this inept response.

'Sorry!' she blazed. 'You sound it, I must say! Now get out of here before I call someone to throw you out.'

'I'm going,' he said coolly. 'It's all right.'

'You ought to be ashamed,' she said bitterly.

'I am,' he said. 'What do you think? I was cut out for something better. My poor old Ma' — his tone was indescribably cynical as he said this — 'would turn in her grave if she knew what I had come to. Still, you can't really blame me, can you? The way I look at it is you owe me something for this leg a mine. Injury sustained while looking after your interests. Like industrial employment benefits,' he explained.

She stared at him, pig-eyed with suspicion.

'What are you getting at? It wasn't only me you fought for.'

'It wasn't only me fought, come to that. But here we are, you and me, and if I take something from you — not much compared with a leg, you have to admit: you oughter study the insurance rates! — still, it does sort of even things up a bit. How else d'you expect me to live? I'm no clerk. Sheep-farming and soldiering, that's all I know; and I'm no good for either of them anymore. They taught me to *knit* in hospital! It's enough to make you laugh; if it don't make you cry! But, Christ, lady, how do they expect me to *live*? On my disability pension and what they give you for a V.C.?'

'Are you a V.C.?'

'V.C. and M.M. Got the M.M. in Catania and the V.C. in Arnhem, where I also got this,' he said, touching his leg. He watched her face and smiled crookedly, 'You don't believe me.' He pulled the medals from his pocket and held them out to her, dangling in his palm. 'And in case you're wondering what kind of a soldier it is who carries his medals around with him in his pants as a sort of boney fidees, I'd been trying to raise the wind on 'em before I happened along your street. Funny to think I traded my home and land and job, and my right leg, too, for these, and I can't even raise half a nicker on 'em. So it turns out, I'm the mug!'

'If you've won the V.C.,' said the woman, 'you ought to be all the more ashamed of what you're doing now. My advice to you is, don't try it again. You mightn't have the luck next time to hit on a woman who lost her soldier at Dunkirk. People don't feel about soldiers now the way they did during the war.'

'Lady,' he said earnestly, 'that's God's own truth you've spoken there!' He gave her his mirthless thin-lipped grin. 'Well, so long . . . and, thanks.'

She heard him clattering down the steps with obstinate perseverance, and suddenly ran after him, fumbling in her bag.

'Soldier!' she called. 'Wait! . . . Just for luck,' she said with sentimental good will, pressing the note into his palm.

He could have pushed in her bloody ugly old face! Tears of rage and humiliation blurted into his eyes. He scrunched the paper convulsively in his hand. He could not trust himself to speak. She patted his shoulder sympathetically, half in tears herself.

He swung off, stumble-dumble, out of sight, tears falling, blinding him, running down his chin. He shook with passion. *God strike blind the bloody bitch!* he screamed to himself. *Does she take me for a beggar?*

He caught sight of a child staring as he passed and wanted to fling the ten shillings at him to express his contempt. He had to force himself to restrain the impulse. That also did not help to lessen the humiliation.

Once out of sight round the corner, he folded his crutches into a neat little affair like a wooden shooting stick, and marched off, a trim soldierly figure with a jaunty little swagger, forever marching down the interminable vistas of residential roads.

2

People Don't Feel about Soldiers the Way They Did During the War

In the stuffy urinal, the air greenish, dank, and dim, filled with the steely clangor of banging doors and the clatter of boots over the brown dripping floor, he prepared himself for his next venture. For the day's work was but begun. This man pursued his ends with relentless patience. Now he pulled from his pocket a small red tin containing a cheap blend of pig's lard and vaseline and began to smear the cleansing cream thinly over his face. With womanish absorption he stared at the image in the square of mirror with its look of sickly sweat. He splashed his face from the tap and the water clung in droplets to the grease like beads of perspiration. He was aware in the corner of his eye of a dark blot against the cracked white tiles, the attendant watching him. So he fumbled in his pocket for a coin and slid it modestly among the other coins in the saucer, two of which vanished between his fingers. Thomas Bates never minded giving if he could be sure of getting the money back twice over.

Then off again, pausing in likely districts to simulate faintness or anguish. Reciting his piece like a gypsy, with the same perfected automatic phrases, and, like a gypsy, picking up what he could, here and there.

Later, hunched on a lumpy lodging house bed, he would examine his trophies, turning them over and over in his fingers curiously, like a savage, searching for the invisible signs that would betray to him their true value. What rudiments he had picked up from the trade only led him to believe that all geese, if white, must be swans.

Then having noted down every particular in a little book, he would divide them into lots and make them up into parcels, enclosing a cunning letter, in the tidy unconvincing copperplate he had been taught in the Institution. These would then be dispatched to various shabby jewelers' shops around London. In this instance, a parcel consisting of part of a set of carved pearl-handled fruit knives and forks; a pair of silver saltcellars; an ashtray of some whitish, semi-opaque substance that Bates fondly hoped was white jade; and a miniature of a boy, angelically fair, in a red jacket and frilled shirt was accompanied by a letter in this style, the heading set out in a very businesslike way, and then:

Dear Sir,

Thinking the enclosed might interest you to purchase. The Miniature has been in my Family for a number of years which is reputed to be a likeness of the poet Shelley when a child. Please note, the salt-sellers are Georgian. Some years ago a Collector offered £25 for the little bowl, it being what is called Muttonfat Jade, which I refused at the time. I regret the fruit-service is incomplete owing to a Robbery (here a convulsion of silent laughter shook a nasty blot on to the page). Kindly address remittance for same to Frederick Noble, Esq., Poste Restante, Worthing . . .

Even the cost of package and postage would be scrupulously noted in his little book. Oh, every item was kept in this minute ledger with the greatest attention. For to Bates this was his 'business,' and anything with figures enchanted him. He could not be too methodical, too serious, about the proper conduct of his affairs. By sheer effort of mind he had kept himself from the disorderly realms dwelt in by his kind. Not for him the phony glamour of the 'tough guy' or the 'flash type,' he had never aspired to be a 'wide boy,' indeed he shuddered away from all such dangerous obviousness. He was a model Institution boy, had absorbed their training through his pores and in his queer, crooked, heartless way was as sober and diligent and meticulous as they could wish. He cherished a mad dream of some miraculously steady and respectable life with unlimited money in the bank to be spent exclusively on his adored self, to be lavished on his un-thwarted and richly, enviously, esteemed self. But, poor fellow, he lacked the brains and vitality to attain these ends, lacked even the ambition to attempt it. For he had discovered while still a lad that the one thing he could not *bear* was work. To be compelled to take orders sent him fairly frantic, made him feel he must *split in two* or escape into a fit or something (indeed, at the electrician's he was first apprenticed to, they took him for an epileptic). Partly because of this and partly because of his resentment and distrust of other people, he was probably the only crook in England not engaged in the black market. All that remained open to him, then, was a life of industrious petty crime.

For days, hanging about Worthing, waiting for his remittance, Bates was haunted by the warning that woman had flung out in casual spite: 'People don't feel about soldiers now the way they did during the war.' The hateful truth of it was constantly revealing itself to him. Barely nine months since all fronts closed down, and already his business was falling to pieces. People no longer glowed with sympathetic curiosity at sight of a wounded soldier; they looked the other way, to avoid his demands on their dried-up wells of compassion. It made him boil with indignation to find how little people appreciated the true nature of a soldier's sacrifice. He'd have been a mug all right if he'd let himself get blown to bits for a rotten lot like them. And Thomas Bates was not a mug. So he faced squarely enough the admission that the days of his racket were numbered.

He was never an agile thinker; a man of small imaginations and prudent ventures, his rackets were as laboriously worked out as a dancer's routine, all hard thought and muscular precision. To fit his dance to another tune required more wit than he commonly possessed.

So what was to be done? He brooded over the problem one icy June day, hugging his knees on a breakwater, with a livid sea cut by the wind into countless scars of foam. The world was roofed in with heavy slate-hued clouds, lumbering behind the wheeling gulls as they raced shrieking inshore. The beach was deserted, except for a few children challenging from time to time the birds with their excited screams; or, here and there, a solitary swimmer bobbing among the waves.

He pitched his fag butt viciously at a swooping gull. The water, slapping with irritable insistence against the stone breakwater beneath him, was the color of dish water, with a scum of foam drifting. He watched the fag end split and disintegrate. A woman swirled and wallowed into his field of vision, staring straight up at him from sea-drenched eyes, her mouth open, washed over by waves. One arm plunged into the air in a legendary gesture.

He watched her without attention. With the insistence of Fate her face came out of the waves again, her desperate eyes still fastened on his. The mouth, spouting water like a sculptured fountain, belched out a choked cry.

(*Help!* called the gulls. *Help!* . . . *Help!* . . . And the wind swept up the children's cries of laughter into Valkyrie screams . . .)

Again a hand thrust out of the sea. Like

a marble shriek. He frowned with annoyance at being distracted from his profane meditations. As though anyone could drown in about three feet of water! It was too absurd! The fool had simply lost her head.

So Bates disliked her from the first.

Perhaps if there had been no one else in sight, he would have continued to ignore her. But it was too near the shore for him to dare do that. Crossly he unlaced his shoes and removed his outer clothes. It was extremely provoking, extremely distasteful to have to drop into that dirty bitter sea. He stood irresolute, the wind teasing his shirttails, exposing his buttocks. Then he lowered himself into the water till the waves sucked chillingly round his waist, and caught hold of the woman to pull her up. But even with his aid, she floundered in his grasp, and fell, and clutched him weakly with her nails, hanging from his neck, half-strangling him. He could feel his own feet slipping, the shingle sliding from under them, giddily. He shifted from heel to heel more and more rapidly, on the point of losing balance, when she blessedly righted herself; and for a moment they clung in a strange embrace, their naked legs entwined. Then he lugged the creature up the beach to sprawl on a bank of stones beside the deserted bathing huts and heave up half the ocean from her inside.

He pulled up his trousers, fastened his shoes, shivering in his clammy garments. The woman had not stirred and he reluctantly went across to her. She was alive all right; she was shuddering.

'You all right?'

She sat up, smeary and blubber faced, a few loose strands of hair marbling her mottled flesh. She exclaimed incredulously through trembling lips, 'I nearly drowned . . . I nearly drowned.' There were salt tracks on her face like frozen tears.

'Well, it's no good hanging about here doing a monologue about it. You want to buck up and get some clothes on and a hot drink inside you. And the same goes for me too, I might add.'

'You saved my life!'

'And I'm trying to save it again; unless

you're mad keen to get pneumonia. Come on, where are your clothes? Buck up, do!' he said impatiently.

'Look what I've done to my foot! I think it's broken. Oh, goodness!'

He bullied her into hobbling as far as her hut.

'You will wait for me?' she begged.

'You'll be all right now,' he assured her.

'Oh, I won't. Please! I'm awfully upset, and besides how am I to get home with this foot of mine?'

'Well, I can't carry you; so what?'

'That's not a very nice way to speak,' she said tearfully.

'Oh, for God's sake, get a move on, then!' he screamed. 'Do you want me to catch my death of cold, hanging about for you? That's a fine reward, I must say!'

'But I won't be a minute, I swear,' she said hurriedly, banging shut the door. 'Nearly ready . . . Won't be half a tick now,' she called out encouragingly from time to time.

'Hurry up!' he grumbled. 'Don't mind making a nuisance of yourself, I must say.'

But when she at last emerged, he was obliged to admit that she had turned out to be not at all a bad-looking wench and much younger than he had supposed. She was a big well-built girl, and her bare legs beneath the pink cotton dress were brown and sturdy. Her hair, released from the rubber cap, spread in a wiry golden-brown bush round her head, like bright rays shining from the sun of her face. Her eyes were gray, the whites like china, sculpted in their sockets. Her mouth was big and shapeless, a soft naked pink against her brown skin.

She had on a faded crimson cardigan over the pink dress, and she had somehow crammed her bruised foot into her canvas sandals. Under one arm she carried a shabby fawn handbag, and her bathing things in an orange plastic carryall.

She said breathlessly, 'I wasn't long, was I?'

'Long enough.'

'Oh, I *wasn't*.'

'Still you look a bit more human now, I will say.'

'I've got to thank you,' she said shyly,

'for saving my life. If you hadn't been there I don't know what would have happened, really.'

'You'd have drowned,' he said, bored.

'That's what I mean: you saved my life.'

'People didn't ought to go bathing in weather like this if they can't swim,' he said severely.

'I can swim,' she said excitedly. 'What happened was my foot got caught somehow under the breakwater, and I couldn't get it out again, I don't know why. And while I was standing on one leg trying to free it, a wave came along and knocked me over and then I couldn't get up again, and when I tried to call, the waves — '

'Well, you'd better pop off home, if you've got a home, and get a hot drink inside you, I should say. You look a sight!'

'Do I? How?' she said crestfallen, touching her hair with uncertain fingers. 'That's because I didn't look in the glass, so as not to keep you waiting. It's your fault then, if I look a sight.'

'You're looking a bit green, was my meaning, as if you might pass out. You want some hot tea or something to buck you up. I could do with some myself, if it comes to that.' He said, considering, 'We might go and have a cup, what do you say?'

(Every man by his actions chooses the death he is to die.)

She flushed. 'I ought to go home. They'll be expecting me.'

'Well, you're a big girl now, aren't you?'

She said hesitatingly, 'If you came back with me afterward, you could explain. And then Daddy could thank you too: he'd want to do that.'

Bates almost smiled. 'I might. We'll see.'

Still she hung back. 'Do I really look a sight?' she murmured.

'You're all right.'

'No, tell me the truth! Or are you just saying that?'

'For God's sake,' he cried, goaded, 'what's the matter with you?'

'All right,' she said hurriedly. 'All right. If you're satisfied. Will you take my arm, then? Because I can't properly walk on this foot, only on the heel sort of. Like this,' she said, leaning on him and limping along.

Her unconfined bust jounced softly against his hand with atrocious familiarity. It was something he could not endure, to be touched or caressed; it was an invasion of his privacy; any movement of animal affection must come from him — or at least must come *first* from him. Soft and slug-like the breast yielded against his knuckles nauseatingly. His hand of itself jerked away from the unpleasant contact. He said quickly, 'Here, this place will do,' and led her, hanging on his arm like a bride, into a marble tearoom as big as a Khan's palace.

'Here's a table,' she murmured. 'Or here.'

But no, none of the vacant tables would do. 'Wait,' he said, firmly propelling her through the maze of tables to the strains of the 'Barcarolle,' 'we'll find a better one.'

But in the end he decided on a table for four, at which a woman was already seated, reading a book in a brown paper cover. She glanced up at them briefly, and in a nicely social-minded gesture inched the cruet into the center of the table.

'No, go on, sit there,' said Bates, when the girl made to sit next to him; 'so as I can look at you,' he added, giving her a sideways sultry glance, so that she reddened and flumped down clumsily beside the reading woman.

Bates seated himself opposite and favored her with a long serious stare, till she did not know where to look and busied herself trying to arrange her carryall and handbag comfortably on her thighs (but her heart was beating nervously: 'hero' and 'masterful' ran confusedly in her brain; this was what she had always expected from life. All her ideas about life came from the books she read and the romantic rescue was an integral part of them and therefore by analogy an integral part of life — her favorite novels always started with a romantic rescue, the man always fierce and haughty at first but in the end melted irresistibly by the girl's winning ways. It seemed like Fate. And the way those strange dark eyes of his had sprung to life from their dull inward-gazing trance when he looked at her just now gave her such a queer swoony feeling all over that she knew it must be love, knew it must be what they called 'love at first sight.' She was dizzy with excitement).

'Here,' he said, 'hand us those over and I'll put them on this chair.' And he took her bags from her and settled them on the seat beside him.

She clasped her soft brown hands under her chin and gazed at him fondly.

'You've never even asked my name,' she reproached him gently. 'It's Grace Pickering. What's yours?'

He frowned at her, with a warning glance at her neighbor.

'What's the matter? I must know what your name is, after saving my life.'

'Frederick Noble.'

'Oh, I like that name! I do like that name! It just suits you down to the ground: *Noble!*'

'Here, dry up!' he muttered. 'Anyone'd think you were barmy.'

She looked scared, and shut up.

Gratified at the ease with which he could manage her, he said more kindly,

'Well, Grace, what are you going to order? Excuse *me*,' he said with aggressive civility to the reading woman, and removed the menu card from behind her book.

He made Grace read the items aloud to him, so that while her attention was absorbed and her face hidden in the card, he could pick her purse.

The waitress took their order. The lady who led the orchestra with a violin was playing the 'Caprice Viennoise' with her eyes closed.

'I love this piece, don't you?' Grace yearned, trying to hum it in a variety of keys.

'Can't say I noticed.'

'You staying in Worthing long?'

He shrugged.

'Where do you live, then?'

'What a lot of questions you ask, don't you?'

'I'm sorry, if you don't want to tell me — '

'Can't tell you, my dear kid; because I don't live anywhere. See?'

This puzzled her, but she gave more

consideration to the way he called her his dear kid, which seemed to her very loving, very sweet.

'I expect you've just come out of the Army. Is that it?'

'I was in the Army. But I've just come out of hospital.'

Her eyes grew round with anxiety.

'Bit a shrapnel in me skull. Lucky I've a thick head, eh?' he laughed carelessly.

'Oh, what a terrible thing! And now you're down here, convalescing?'

'Something like that.'

'Have you no family to look after you?'

'No.'

'Oh, that's sad, to have no home!'

'Home is where you make it.'

'You haven't a wife then? Or am I asking too many questions again?'

'No, I haven't a wife.'

Grace smiled, and said, 'More tea?' with the arch gesture her mother used.

Presently he leaned forward and whispered, 'Excuse me a minute, will you? I won't be long.' He walked lightly away. Gone before the sense of his words had penetrated her brain . . .

It was years since he had played that old trick. The table had been chosen not only because he could 'force' her into the seat next to the occupied one, thereby obliging her to hand over her bags and bundles for comfort's sake to him to place on the chair beside him, but also because it was screened from the Gentlemen's and the other exit into Hill Street by the confusing false dichotomy of an enormous sheet of looking glass.

To his rage the girl's purse contained only a few shillings, two grubby peppermints, a canceled 1/6 New Zealand stamp torn from an envelope, and a screwed-up receipt for a registered parcel. Four and threepence halfpenny for jumping into the sea! A nice reward! Saved the bag's life, ruined his own afternoon and that was all he got for his pains.

So that was another reason for Bates to dislike her.

3

Do Dreams Come True?

He never imagined he would see her again. But he was obliged to hang about for his remittances. And in his calculations he left no margin for other people's endeavors. Simply, he usually did not believe in other people, could not believe in them as existing with the same powerful identity as himself.

But Grace Pickering did not forget him. The romance of it all . . . the rescue . . . his somber enigmatic face and his extraordinary un-life-like brutality, so like the unreasonable behavior of the ugly-handsome heroes in the books she read . . . all this *haunted* her mind. It was not for nothing that their paths had crossed. She *knew* she would see him again, because it *was* all 'so like a book,' and Grace never doubted that books were true — in essence, if not in fact — never doubted that all stories ended happily or that love would always 'find a way.'

She lived with her father and mother on the top of Salvington Hill in a little white bungalow with imitation shutters, called 'Blue Windows.' Mr. Pickering was manager of a local branch bank. A tall rather ungainly man with a pale bald face and restless eye muscles. A just man, he never let his daughter see that she was a disappointment to him. Little Mrs. Pickering — 'the long and the short of it' their friends quaintly called them — had a small face that looked sharp and pared away beneath her gaily-dyed hair; there was always a strained look in her pretty blue eyes, and her hands involuntarily made placatory little gestures. It was her religion to count the silver before putting it away after every meal.

Grace was not quite such a fool as to talk about her hero before Mr. Pickering. She knew what he thought.

'You surely don't think *he* stole my purse,' she cried disgustedly to her father after that difficult little contretemps in the tea shop.

'My poor Grace,' her father had said, twitching his forehead, blinking, 'you really should endeavor from time to time to use your mind.'

But to her mother she rehearsed the events of that day endlessly. They had so little to talk about those two, together all the day long, that this loomed as something interesting and important. And, 'Mumples,' she would beseech, 'you do believe I shall see him again, don't you? You do believe in some way it was meant?'

No wonder that after a little this unknown figure began to skulk in Mrs. Pickering's dreams. To both of them dreams were tremendously significant, esoteric. Sometimes Mrs. Pickering's dreams had come true. In this one, the dark figure had crept out of a hole in Mr. Pickering's sock, and Mrs. Pickering had been afraid her husband would notice him, but somehow he slipped invisibly behind Mrs. Pickering and murmured over her shoulder that he wanted to marry Grace; only he insisted it must be at a registry, by which she knew he meant a bathing hut, and again was alarmed, apprehending that would mean Grace must be wed naked; at which he leaned over her intimately and gave her a tender, immodest caress, saying in a voice that she dreaded would rouse her husband's attention, 'But we understand these things; you'll be on my side, won't you?' so that she was overcome, with suspicion of him at this cajolery, and the pang of sweet pleasure she felt at his touch, and shame for herself at feeling this pleasure, and indignation that he should so caress her in front of her husband and daughter.

So it was not an easy dream to describe to Grace. Yet a little of it had to be told to relieve the cloud of oppression under which she had wakened.

The little she heard was enough to excite Grace. She pored over the dream book, looking up 'weddings,' 'bathing huts,' and 'socks.' It was very puzzling.

'But, Mumples,' said Grace earnestly, puckering her unlined brow, 'do dreams come true, or do they go by contraries?'

When she saw him, just a glimpse of him crossing South Street, that same afternoon, her heart gave quite a lurch. She ran after him, plunging into the traffic.

His arm was like steel in her grasp; the face he turned to her, as darkly frowning, as guarded, as a castle keep. But she was so pleased to see him, so pleased he had not left, as she had feared, that she blurted out oafishly she'd been looking for him everywhere.

He stared coldly.

She said, 'But you can't have forgotten me! Saving my life, and then us having tea together, all that! I've wondered so, what you must have thought of me going off like that, without waiting for you to come back; only it was so late and I knew Mumples would be anxious . . . '

'I remember you,' he said. 'I remember you now.'

'I did wait, but you were such a long time. I couldn't think what had happened to you; began to think you must have fallen down the drain,' she laughed, and then wondered if she'd been coarse.

He said sullenly, 'It's my head. I told you I'd just come out of hospital. I get turns. Everything goes blank. When I come to I don't remember anything.'

'You're not fit to go about alone,' she declared pityingly.

She was still holding his sleeve, still standing close to him, gazing into his face with a wide dithery grin. She began to talk in a loud self-conscious voice with whickers of boisterous, excited laughter. It was dreadful. Everyone on the street was turning to stare.

He pulled his sleeve away. 'We can't stand here,' he muttered.

'Let's have an ice, let's go and have an ice at Korg's. I'd like that. Oh, come on! It's only across the road.'

'I can't. I've got a date.'

'Where?'

'The other end of the town, if it's any business of yours. And I'm late as it is, talking to you.'

'All right, I'll come part of the way with you, if you like,' she offered.

'What for?' he asked coldly.

'Company.'

'I got no quarrel with my own company, thanks. Besides — I told you — I'm in a hurry.' His face was peevish and somehow dangerous.

So was hers dangerous, the mouth squared at the corners like a child's.

'You needn't speak so unkindly,' she quavered in a voice that went high and trembled ominously. She could not bear not to be the loved one of all the world.

He watched in horror, in desperation.

'Don't blub! For Crissake! All right, all right; come if you want to. What do I care?'

'But I don't want to come with you if you don't *want* me,' she explained, hurrying along at his side. Only, there was so much to tell him, now that he was found again. She was anxious that he should meet Daddy, Mumples, anyway.

'Who's Mumples?'

'Mumples is my mother, it's what I call her. I've told her all about you, and she had such a funny dream about you creeping out of a hole in my father's sock. Do you believe in dreams?'

'You'd no right,' he said crossly. 'I don't care for that sort of thing.'

'It was only a dream,' Grace protested. 'A person can't help what she dreams. I won't tell you the rest then, if that's how you go on.'

'I'm not referring to that. What I don't like is being discussed with other people.'

'But, gracious me, you couldn't mind me telling Mumples! I had to tell Mumples. Where's the harm in her knowing? She is very grateful to you, she's longing to meet you!'

'I don't like it, that's all. It makes me nervous. Like being watched when you think you're alone.'

'Well, don't walk so fast! Don't you want to hear about the rest of the dream?'

'No,' he said bluntly.

'Well, what do you want me to tell you, then?'

'Must you tell me anything?'

'Oh, you are disagreeable! I don't know what makes you so short. I don't see why you can't be friendly to a person. You don't behave a bit like someone who's rescued someone, I must say.'

There was a pause. And then she remembered to tell him she had lost her purse the day she met him, and how cross Daddy had been with her, because he always *said* she was not to be trusted with money and he would never allow her even to keep her own Savings Book.

At that, he looked at her quite amiably and asked, as if he were really interested, 'Are they your own savings? I mean, because that would be a rotten trick, if you've saved up the money yourself.'

'Well, no, not exactly,' she said, delighted at his interest, recollecting that last time it had taken him a long while to warm up and become friendly. 'It's money that Daddy has saved for me, for every year of my life he puts a pound away on my birthday. He says he won't be able to afford it much longer, me getting older this way every year,' she laughed.

'Get on!' he said. 'You're not old. What are you: eighteen? Twenty?'

Her laugh neighed out rapturously. 'Well, you work it out,' she said. 'I've got put away four hundred and sixty-five pounds . . . Really I've got four hundred and eighty-two altogether, but that's including other presents I've put away.'

He said in genuine astonishment, 'You're never *thirty!* I can't hardly believe

44

it. I took you for a kid!'

Now his attention was quite different; his glance persevered over her like a snail.

Grace said dizzily, 'How ever did you work it out so quickly? I don't know how you could! You must be good at mental arithmetic!'

'Oh, I am,' he said waggishly, taking her arm, in sudden high spirits. 'I'm a wizard with figures. With some more than others. A figure like yours, f'instance' — he squeezed her arm against his side — 'gives me all sorts of ideas! You'd be surprised!'

But, 'I don't like that sort of talk,' she demurred with virgin delicacy, pulling her arm away. 'You ought not to say things like that.'

'Well, I never,' he declared, 'you're a funny sort of girl, not wanting a chap to tell you you've caught his fancy! Five minutes ago you were all over me,' he said huffily.

'It was you that changed,' said Grace bravely.

'Well, go on, then; why did I?'

'I don't know,' she murmured weakly,

not liking to say what she thought.

'It was when you told me how much money you had and I guessed your age, wasn't it? Well, then? I thought you were just a silly kid before; as soon as I found out you were a woman, I felt different, see? I don't like mucking about with kids. And the more they got what it takes' — he sketched a voluptuous form on the air — 'the more they scare me. That's why I kept trying to push you off, baby!' he said with gross familiarity.

'You mean, you did . . . like me, really, all the time?'

His eyes slid round till they met hers . . . like dark stones, they were, pressing into hers. Her legs felt filleted, useless. He made some cheap quip in the cinematic mode, which she hardly heard and could never afterward recall. For, it was queer, she no longer liked him so much, had somehow taken fright, wanted to escape.

She stammered, 'I think I've come far enough now,' recollecting her duties and the weight of the shopping bag on her arm. 'Goodbye!' she said, and scuttled away.

(Every man by his actions chooses the death he is to die.) He called after her casually, 'Meet me outside the Lido, tonight, eight o'clock.'

And smiled to himself cheerfully, knowing she'd be there.

4

I'm Never to See You Again

Bates had no qualms about how to woo her. She'd do all the running herself. Like a ripe mulberry dropping off a tree into his mouth. The first break he'd had in months. This was a racket he had worked before — squeezing savings out of poor innocents on one pretext or another. Some of them he had married (never in his own name, for that would have seemed too legal, too permanent) but that was not a role that suited him; he loathed the sensation of being 'tied up to' another person, even temporarily. He would not go to such lengths with this fool. He would not need to. To give a little kick to the thing he swore he wouldn't spend more than five bob on her.

These mild summer nights it was a cinch. Though it didn't do to be ostentatious about his miserliness. Sometimes he treated her to a coffee or an ice. The 'pictures,' he said made his head ache; so when Grace was tired of walking or chilled with sitting humped on the beach with his arm round her he would spend a few pence on a bus ride, sitting up in front where it was warm, like lovers, her head dreamily on his shoulder, lulled for once from her wearisome chatter. Then, now and again, in the humming silence, he could drop into her head one of his suggestions.

Nevertheless, at the end of five days he had failed to persuade her to hand over her Savings Book. So he quarreled with her (a classic proof that it does not take two to make a quarrel) and said he never wanted to see her again.

Grace went home, white-faced. She could not see what she had done wrong. What made her trouble more grievous was, that for reasons she herself could hardly fathom, she had not told her parents who it was she was meeting every evening; she had lied to them, pretending she was going to a cinema or meeting friends. Now it was difficult to confess the truth. Now it was difficult not to confess the truth, with so much distress weighting her bosom, and the longing for advice . . . For she still did not know where he lived and she feared she had lost him forever.

Then when she had quite lost heart came the anonymous letter, hand-printed on very thin ruled paper:

IF YOU WANT TO KNOW WHAT YOUR BOYFRIEND IS UP TO GO DOWN TO THE PIER TONIGHT AND SEE FOR YOURSELF.

It was not easy to shake off Mumples, who perhaps at last was suspicious, and when Grace said she felt like going to a film, said she did too. Grace only got away alone by hurting Mumples' feelings. So that, poor girl, she was all agitation and remorse as she hurried down Salvington Hill; she had such a good nature.

It was cold hanging about the pier entrance and she thought people were nudging each other and giving her funny looks. It belatedly occurred to her that the letter might be a practical joke (by whom perpetrated though, she had no idea).

And then she saw him. She almost didn't recognize him, through the tears in her eyes. She almost didn't recognize him, because she had never seen him laughing before.

A rowdy, loose-lipped kid about fifteen was hanging on his arm, shrieking with mirth. Her showy bracelets jangled, and her mouth was a splotch of raspberry paint. She waved a hat in the air hilariously. She might have been drunk.

Frederick's eyes looked right through Grace, as if he had not seen her. That she could not bear. That gave her the spurt of courage to run after him; touch his arm.

'Freddy!'

'Hullo,' he said, not nicely, but halting his companion all the same.

'Freddy . . . I want to speak to you.'

'Well you can't now; you can see I'm with a lady.' And then relenting, 'See you tomorrow, if you like. Or meet you here in an hour's time, if you'll still be hanging around.'

'All right. I'll wait.'

'Who's she?' Grace heard the child ask as they moved away. She didn't hear him answer, 'My sister,' but she heard the girl's obscene yell of laughter, and the blood burned under her skin.

Daylight fled from the beach first. People could embrace in the dusk-filled hollows, or among the weed-dank piles under the pier, or in musty interstices between the serried bathing huts; Bates knew all the ways of making love without spending a penny. He would have been aghast at the notion: money for that! Some bags thought you were doing them a favor if you gave them a poke in the angle of two walls. And so you were.

This kid, though, had the impudence to ask him for money. He was feeling so good-humored over Grace that he merely slapped her meager buttocks and said, 'Get along with you!'

'Come on, ducky, don't be mean! I gave you a good time, didn't I?'

'You ought to be ashamed of yourself, asking for money,' he declared indignantly. 'Why, you're nothing but a dirty little trollop!'

'Here, what's the idea, you dirty crook?' she cried, thrusting a knee threateningly between his. 'Who you calling names? You bloody well hand over two quid or I'll bloody well call a copper. I'm under age, I am; I'm fifteen, 'n I can prove it!'

Bates gave her one good hard slap across the face, so that her head banged painfully against the side of the hut and she began to whimper.

'Your dad ought to smack your back-side for you, carrying on like this at your age,' he told her virtuously, and left her, weeping with temper and pain, groveling among the stones in the dark for her lipstick, her comb, all the wretched little tools of her trade . . .

In spite of his good temper, he was suddenly annoyed to see Grace waiting for him so patiently and to feel her arm goose-fleshed with cold, and he opened at once by saying crossly, 'What were you doing down here? Spying on me?'

This was so near the truth that Grace was too taken aback to answer.

'I thought you didn't like young girls,'

she remarked in a meek but puzzled voice.

'Oh my god,' he cried, throwing up his arms extravagantly, 'defend me from jealous women! She's just a kid staying at my hotel I was trying to do a good turn to.'

'I thought you seemed to be enjoying yourself.'

'Well, you don't expect me to sit at home and mope just because you turned me down, did you?'

'But it was you who said you didn't want to see *me* again,' she protested.

'Well, what was the use? I don't know why you want to see me now, if it comes to that?'

'I just . . . wanted to see . . . wondered . . . whether we couldn't be . . . friends?'

'It seems a bit late for that. I'm going away. I'm fed up with Worthing,' he said petulantly.

'Oh, Freddy!' she wailed.

★   ★   ★

Three minutes later he asked her to marry him. She had never received a proposal of marriage before so it did not seem to her particularly inept or chillily expressed. She was quite overborne with rapture at this sudden reversing of her limitless despair.

She lifted her head from his shoulder to whisper, 'What will Daddy and Mumples say?' incredulously.

'I shall have to ask your old man's permission of course,' he said in a straightforward, manly way. 'You'll have to arrange for me to come up to the house and meet him. D'you think we'll get on? Funny old cove, is he? Or on the sharp side?'

'Daddy's a bit sharp, but he doesn't mean anything by it. He'll love you, dearest, of course he will,' she reassured herself.

It was a little too crude even for Thomas Bates, to bounce straight in and announce that he meant to marry their daughter. A certain finesse was obviously necessary. He put it into Grace's mind, and a few days later he was invited to tea at 'Blue Windows' to meet Mrs. Pickering.

Mumples could hardly believe Grace's romantic tale; she was in a flutter of nervous excitement and obscure terrors. But the instant she saw him, all her high anticipations vanished; his jauntily sinister figure killed stone dead the image of a sensible man between forty and fifty years of age, probably a widower, seeking comfort and affection, a responsible, kindly man, patient with her girl's mistakes.

The fringed lashes on his pale cheek made him look delicate, and to a motherly person there was something pathetic as well as disappointing in the shoddy blue suit and shirt none too clean at the cuff. Even that he was quite common could be forgiven. But eyes and mouth and hands betrayed him; the fixed, dark, pupil-less eyes so like a snake's, the rattrap of a mouth, and the short, thick-fingered hand of a butcher. And his dreadful self-assurance, that took Grace's doting for granted.

Mumples felt a chill at the heart she could not account for, or explain to her husband, or wholly conceal from Grace, who (once her lover had taken his departure) excitedly asked Mumples what she thought about him.

Bates, however, was well satisfied with the result of the tea party, and spent hours in his lodgings preparing confusing financial statements for Mr. Pickering's austere eye.

★　★　★

The interview with Mr. Pickering, Bates hemmed against the dining table by a chain of leather chairs, was not pleasant. Mr. Pickering's pale eye was austere indeed.

He let Bates run on, asked him a few questions, led him into a trap once or twice and watched him wriggle out, and himself said nothing, but sat there, the nerves twitching beneath the skin spasmodically.

'You have not known my daughter very long, it appears. Are you aware that she has no means of her own?'

'It's not a subject Grace and I have discussed. She did happen to mention, I believe, that she has a few hundreds in a savings account.'

'Ah, I rather thought she would have told you that! And may one inquire, how you propose to keep her?'

'I don't anticipate much difficulty there; once my invention is on the market.'

'Ah? You're an inventor?'

'Well, no, I wouldn't like to say that. My life's been spent in the saddle, like I told you. But I did have the luck, if you like to call it that, to hit on a new process solution for cleaning clothes. You know the type of thing, like this bottled benzene stuff, only that isn't any good. But my stuff, well, it'll remove pretty well anything, grease, dirt, fruit stains, ink stains . . . Of course, if it interested you, I'd be only too pleased to go into it in detail. Matter of fact I've got a sample on me; thought you might like to see it,' he said nonchalantly. He brought out a chemist's one-ounce bottle which he had filled with Thawpit, and offered it to Mr. Pickering.

But Mr. Pickering said plainly that all

he was interested in was to learn how Mr. Noble proposed to market it.

'Ah! Now that's where you might be able to help me with your line of business. I've got to find someone to put up the money first of all. I've worked it all out. To give you an idea, look at this!' And he thumbed over some grubby sheets of paper covered with columns of figures in pounds, shillings and pence, multiplied and divided all over the page. It was very impressive as a piece of industry; but Mr. Pickering did not even spare it a glance. Bates, unperturbed by this lack of enthusiasm, was turning over pages, and expounding with the aid of a choppy forefinger the significance of the figures. According to the figures, at any rate one would make 700 per cent profit on every bottle sold.

'I think any businessman would consider that a fair profit. If you put up £500, I reckon I should be able to pay you back in two years. Or if you preferred you could buy a share in it. I don't reckon myself a businessman, but if I had the chance of a proposition like this, I should think myself a mug if I turned it down.' He leaned back with a satisfied smile; manipulating figures always intoxicated him.

But Mr. Pickering was not so easily intoxicated. 'And where is the money coming from to keep my daughter, meanwhile? Or am I supposed to finance that too?' he asked with a smile that showed his big white teeth like prehistoric stumps.

Bates said quickly, 'If I didn't pay you back right away and we could draw two hundred a year from capital to begin with for our personal expenses, then I reckon — '

'Rubbish, rubbish, sir! You are asking me to finance your marriage. And in order to disguise its blatancy you put up this impudent rigmarole . . . I think we may as well terminate this unprofitable interview.' The nerves round his eyes jumped and he blinked convulsively.

'You mean you're not going to help?'

'Did you really imagine I would?' He said quite affably. 'The last thing I should dream of would be to encourage my poor daughter to ally herself with a penniless rogue.' He stood up. 'And now I think you'd better go.'

'Me, fighting for the likes of you and getting blown up, and then you calling me a rogue; that's good, I must say!' declared Bates in a rage. 'I'd remind you there's such a thing as a law of libel. Calling people names! And your girl so dotty to marry me, you ought to be glad. You ought to be thankful, I tell you. I could have taken advantage of her a dozen times, if I hadn't been the right sort.'

Mr. Pickering looked suddenly frightening. 'There are more ways than one of taking advantage of a person, Noble. I would draw your attention to the fact. Stealing a girl's purse, for instance; meaner to my mind than seducing her. You don't agree?'

'I don't follow.'

'You surprise me!'

'And I didn't come here to be insulted, either, so if that's your feelings in the matter, I'll take my leave.' He snatched a chair out of the way, glared round the room, and retreated.

'One word more, if you please; a word of warning. If ever I catch you hanging round my daughter again, I shall inform the police. Take heed!'

'I'll remember,' promised Bates, meeting him eye for eye. And swaggered off, undiminished.

As he came out of the dining room into the lounge hall, the door opposite began gently to close.

'Well, Grace!' he said loudly, 'so we're not to be married, after all. Your father's kicking me out!'

Miss Pickering's head appeared round the lintel cautiously, pale-faced, large-eyed.

'Freddy, whatever do you mean?'

'I'm never to see you again. Got that? It seems I'm an adventurer. I've been threatened with the police, if you please!'

'*Freddy!*' she cried in horror. 'Don't go!'

'Grace!' uttered Mr. Pickering, like a monument in the dining-room doorway. 'Clear out, Noble! I've warned you!'

'Well, Grace?' said Bates.

Grace, in terror of both men, wrung

her hands speechlessly.

'You might at least give us a minute alone to say goodbye,' snarled Bates.

Without argument, Mr. Pickering advanced on him with the slow menace of the Commander's statue in *Don Giovanni*. Grace broke into noisy sobs. And under cover of her blusterous weeping, Bates contrived to whisper that he would write to her Poste Restante. 'Did you hear? I'll write to you Poste Restante,' he repeated; and dropping her hands, added aloud, 'Goodbye, Grace. Goodbye, dear. As for you,' he said to Mr. Pickering, 'you'll be hearing shortly from my solicitors.'

5

My Husband Sends His Respects

Lumpy with crying and pale, Grace moped about the house day after day, a reproach to her father, a grief to her mother. Even her mother refused to discuss the sad affair with her but loyally maintained that Daddy knew best. At meals tears would overcome her silently and she would be obliged to leave the table. They would hear her through the wall, sobbing; and the food turned to chaff in their mouths and choked them.

Freddy wrote kindly enough that if she still wanted him to marry her he was willing, but he explained that now, on account of her parents, it would have to be a secret wedding.

Of course they met clandestinely. Clever though he was at letter writing, it needed the magnetism of his presence to steel her to positive action. For one thing, if he was to marry her and take her away he needed money and she would have to find it one way or another. If she couldn't wangle it out of her mother then she must bring him her trinkets or something and he would pawn them for her. If she was shocked at this she was careful not to show it, knowing how impatient he was with her stupid qualms. Even when she had made up her mind to a course of action, she needed to be reassured about it again and again, and yet again. This, Freddy did not understand. When she protested timidly for the umpteenth time that she didn't know if she was doing right, he at once became sharp, on edge with frustration.

'Oh, well, if you don't know your own mind, there's no more to be said. I wouldn't want to persuade you to do anything you think is wrong.'

'But *is* it wrong?'

'Of course you just swallow all the lies your father tells about me. What can I expect? I don't blame you. Pity is I ever let myself get fond of you. All women let you down in the end.'

How pathetic he was! Poor Freddy! He could never realize how much she loved him.

'As if I'd let you down, darling! It's only that I do wonder what Father would do if he found out.'

'What could he do? Nothing. You're free, white and twenty-one, aren't you?'

'But then why must we be married secretly? That's what I don't see.'

'Because if they knew they would try to stop you,' he explained with extreme patience.

'But you said they couldn't,' she wailed, perplexed.

'Look, Grace — I've told you this already — they can't, but they'd try. See? Parents are often like that,' he improvised. 'They get jealous if their children want to leave them.'

'They don't want me to be happy?'

'Well, you've got your own life to live, haven't you? You're not so young any more. You can't sacrifice yourself to them forever.'

Her parents were depressed to find Grace surreptitiously weeping again — just when they had thought she was beginning to get over that man. But Grace wept at the thought of having to run away from home and become a wife all by herself. To steady her nerves and enforce confidence she drew up immensely elaborate schedules for running a house, planning menus and carefully transcribing all the recipes she knew; with silver cleaning, paint washing, linen mending and so on, for every day of the week, as if she was going to be mistress of an establishment twenty times the size of her mother's bungalow.

Bates married her all right. She was Mrs. Frederick Noble, with a gilt ring on her finger and a honeymoon in lodgings in London.

Grace found that being married made you love your husband even more than before. She would not have believed it possible. The very day they arrived, Freddy made her write to her parents so that they should not be anxious. It showed how thoughtful he was, and bore no malice against them. She thought he was wonderful. He even directed what she should say. She knew then that she was as safe with him as she had been at home and she need not have feared that she would have to think for herself now she was a wife.

Dear Father and Mother [she wrote at his dictation],

I write to tell you that I am now married to Mr. Frederick Noble and living in London. We are very happy, so please do not worry about me. We are properly married so please do not worry. Will you please send me my Savings Book as it is mine and in my name and I am entitled to it. I hope you will forgive us soon and have not been worrying.

Ever your loving daughter,
Grace Noble

My husband sends his respects.

'Written by that man!' said Mr. Pickering and tossed the letter across to his wife.

'Oh, no, dear, surely. This is Grace's own writing.'

'Does it sound like Grace? Has Grace ever addressed us as dear father and mother? The man told her what to say. Don't you appreciate the touch about the Savings Book: 'it is in my name and I am entitled to it'?'

To Mrs. Pickering it seemed likely enough that now Grace was married this more dignified style of address seemed natural. She read the letter again.

'She sounds quite happy, doesn't she?' she said hopefully.

Mr. Pickering was too disgusted to reply.

'What shall you do, Percy?'

'I shall ignore it. I perceive very well what his scheme is and I will not be committed to it. In all probability, my dear, our daughter will return to us quite soon, in a few weeks anyway, if we remain firm and sensible.'

'Grace come back to us? But, Percy, how dreadful! Don't you think they really are married, then? How dreadful, how dreadful!'

'Whether they are married or not is hardly the point. Indeed, I should not like to have to decide which would be the worse calamity. The grounds on which I premise her return, however, are simply that I cannot believe even Grace could long endure life with a man of that stamp. The vulgarity and illiteracy of this communication are beyond anything I have ever seen.'

★ ★ ★

So the happy couple waited in London in vain. It was only natural then that Freddy should be morose and ratty. Grace quite appreciated that, and herself felt torn guiltily between conflicting loyalties. What was particularly disappointing to her was that they still resided in these dingy lodgings. She knew she would not feel truly married until she kept house in their own little flat — or even two rooms. But when she wailed about it, Freddy oddly replied that it was 'not worthwhile.'

Bates was away for hours at a time. 'On business,' he told Grace. But really because he could not endure to be cooped up alone with her, her soft body leaning against his, her insatiable need to know what he was thinking, to be told, however automatically, that he loved her. And with Grace too it was largely the tedium which made her so dull that in her efforts to promote conversation (like Mumples with Daddy) she could think of nothing but to wonder what he was thinking about, to nag boringly, coyly, 'Do you love me?'

When he was out, there was nothing whatever to do but stare at the oleograph of 'Highland Cattle' and count the blades of grass in the foreground, or try the effect of the gilded poppy-heads in the window instead of the tongue fern. Then she would sink back into her languid voluptuous dreams or read once again right through her favorite woman's weekly.

Bates wrote to Grace's father himself, a high-flown, threatening letter, remarking, in his favorite phrase, that he knew the law and if his wife did not receive her property by return of post he would be reluctantly obliged to put the matter in the hands of his solicitors. He signed himself with a fine flourish, his obedient servant Frederick Noble.

This work of art, too, was ignored.

He had actually to go to a solicitor, grumbling and cursing, before he could dig the money out of the old man. Her father's obstinacy was chalked up as a black mark against Grace. He made her draw out three pounds at once, for their immediate expenses. That she did willingly enough. She was not mean, never having had cause to be. But he had a job to persuade her to withdraw the whole four hundred and eighty quid. Submissive though she was, she rebelled at that.

'Don't you believe in my invention then? Haven't you got faith in me?' he cried indignantly.

'You know I have, darling.'

'Well, how can I market it without a bit of capital? I got to have a place rigged up for a lab, so's I can make experiments. I got an idea I could improve it now, if only I had somewhere to try it out in. And here we are, living on your money all the time. I don't like that. I never thought I'd come down to being dependent on my wife and having to *beg* for every — '

'Oh, Freddy!' Grace began to sob.

'I want us to have a nice little flat somewhere with our own suites, but how are we ever going to get that when, just now, with bad luck and one thing and another, I haven't got a penny to bless myself with.' He leaned his head back on his arms and said dramatically, 'I never had a home.'

'Oh, darling! I didn't mean . . . I only meant not quite all, to keep a bit back in case of emergency. But of course you know best, darling.'

'Well, all right, don't maul me, Grace! You know I hate being mauled . . . No, I don't want to persuade you. If you've got any doubts, I shouldn't do it.'

'But I haven't,' she cried eagerly. 'I want to give it to you. Truly.'

'I wouldn't let you *give* it to me. What do you take me for? It's to be a loan . . . Yes, of course. Then no one can say anything, don't you see. You won't have lost your money, you'll get it all back one day and interest at $4\frac{1}{2}$ per cent besides, so that you'll be *better* off, Grace, do you understand that? Because now you're only getting 2½ per cent in the Post Office.'

'Oh, but Freddy, you mustn't. I'm sure that's not right,' she protested timidly, humbled by this turning of the tables.

'Yes, it's all quite legal; I know the law. And you won't lose a penny by it, will you, so I'm really doing you a favor. See?'

There were still two long weeks to be got through before the money was obtainable. A sheer waste of time and money, in Bates's opinion, but what could he do? He had to stick to Grace and be halfway kind to her, lest she should turn unhappy and run back home. But he grudged the money he spent on her, terribly. So that when she happened to let fall, as her stream-like chatter burbled and meandered, that she had a grandmother living in St. John's Wood, it came on him like a brilliant illumination, 'By Jay, we'll touch the old girl!'

He said playfully, 'Fancy, we been here all this time and you never mentioned you had people so near! You don't seem very proud of your hubby, I must say. Don't want to show him off, do you?'

She twisted round under his hand to look at him. 'I never thought you'd want to be bothered, she's just a poor old lady,' she said apologetically.

'Poor?' he took up sharply.

'She's a cripple with arthritis, that's what I mean.'

'Well, we'll go and cheer her up,' he promised, lightly pinching Grace's broad cheek.

Grace was pleased to note that her husband was merrier than he had been for days. Bates calculated that the very least the old girl could fork out was a tenner, and she might be good for considerably more. Marriage of one's granddaughter was a sentimental occasion, wasn't it? Even if the wedding had been a bit *sub rosa*, as they say.

Yet the meeting was not a success. The big gloomy house that had already a musty smell of the grave, the old lady fretful and irascible with pain, and the domineering companion lowered their spirits. They sat in the muffled Edwardian drawing room on two upright chairs opposite the old lady, like schoolchildren, answering her sharp uncompromising questions. Behind her the whiskery companion clicked steel needles. Bates's jocosities did not sound well in that place, before these grim old women. He stood up, 'Excuse me, will you?'

'Heckie will show you the cloakroom,' said the old woman.

'That's all right, I'll find it,' he said quickly.

'Heckie, go with him!'

'Don't bother!'

'This way,' commanded the companion, marching before him.

He spent an age in there, pulling the plug, running water in the basin; but when he came out she was still there, waiting for him. He was furious.

Moreover, there was no mention of a check, no money tucked cosily into one's palm, nothing but the dry query, 'What do you want for a wedding present?'

And when Grace murmured, 'Oh, nothing, Granny, you mustn't bother,' she only said wearily, 'Think about it and let me know.'

'You mustn't talk anymore,' said Miss Hector firmly. 'You're worn out.'

'Yes, take me away, Heckie,' she sighed. And received Grace's kiss in silence, the silence of exhaustion.

Directly they were out of earshot, he said, 'Well, Grace, go and wash your hands and we'll go home.'

Surprised, Grace declared she did not need to wash her hands.

'Do as I tell you,' he snarled, and she hurried to obey.

When Miss Hector returned to say that Mrs. Pickering of course expected them to stay to tea if they would kindly excuse her from being present herself, Bates countered her suspicious look with an impudent stare.

'We won't stay, many thanks. Grace is just putting on her things. The old lady seems to be in a pretty bad way, doesn't she?'

'She's good for another ten years,' Miss Hector replied sharply. 'So don't you go getting ideas in your head, you nasty bit of work, you,' she as good as added, by the expression on her face.

But every man by his actions chooses the death he is to die, and after he'd gone they discovered the knickknacks missing, though what could they do about it then? However, it caused old Mrs. Pickering to alter her will. She had left Grace a fifth of her estate. Now, so deeply — and rightly, as it happened — did she mistrust the man her granddaughter had eloped with, that she had the capital sum put In Trust for Grace so that she could only use the interest in her lifetime (though it seemed to her only fair the girl should be allowed the general power to will the capital as she pleased), thus safeguarding her money from the depredations of an unscrupulous husband. As far as Bates was concerned she needn't have troubled, he was only living for the day when he could lay his hands on Grace's savings and walk out.

6

Don't Let Anyone Turn You Against Me, Grace

Bates now began to elaborate a fiction about some businessmen up in Manchester who were supposed to be interested in financing his invention to prepare Grace a little for the next move. The next move was where he moved out. With her savings of course. He disappeared the very same day that he went to the Post Office to collect the money.

By evening, Grace in an absolute state of nerves flew to the door when she heard steps, but it was only a letter for her — from her loving husband.

Dear Grace [she read through the tears in her eyes],
You had better go back to your parents. [Oh! she put her hand to her heart like a girl in the films, and sat

down.] The Gentlemen I have spoken to you of want me to discuss important matters with them in Manchester. I could not let you know before as I did not know myself. Hoping you will not be too upset. When things are more settled I will send for you to join me, but I do not wish my Wife alone in London and also it would be a waste of money. I will pray night and day to God to unite our loving hearts once again, as is ever my fond hope. Do not let anyone turn you against me Grace. I will write as soon as I am more settled.

Ever your devoted husband,
F. Noble

It was a terrible blow! She wept. But she had always to be obedient to someone, and what else could she do, poor Grace, but scuttle back to her parents? She had been married just five weeks and two days. It was fully three months before she gave up expecting to hear from him.

★　★　★

Bates held all the wealth of the Indies in his coarse-fingered puds. This not very large sum represented to him immense riches, opening up every avenue of self-gratification. He was as inflated as a frog.

On the one hand, his congenital avarice could hardly bear to let go of a single note, and on the other, he could not resist showering presents on himself — votive offerings at the shrine of his idol. For once his darling self should have everything money could buy.

The voluptuous delight of silk against the skin thrilled him more than any human caress he had ever known. Fine socks, elegant shoes, a twenty guinea suit, why should he not have all these delights? (But it was torture to see the money vanish.)

Four hundred he kept intact. That was not to be squandered. That was to 'settle' him. That was to buy him a little 'property.' For property represented — oh, heavens! — all that was solidly prosperous in this world, and a lavish indolence was the property-owner's way of life.

He pored over the advertisements in

Dalton's Weekly with a stubby forefinger. He might have been striving for the key to Biblical prophecy, sitting there in his braces with his head in his hands, or making immense calculations down the margins with a smudgy inch of pencil.

He trudged through one slum after another, scraping at plaster, pulling off rotten skirting boards, poking sagging ceilings.

At last he found a pair of derelict workmen's dwellings. All that remained of a row that was now just a heap of rubble. They were atrocious, with their peeling plaster, empty windows and rusty iron-work; leaning shakily together like a pair of seedy old drunkards. To think of human beings living in such squalor would have sickened any soul but Bates. All they represented to *him* was a return of 33 per cent per annum on four hundred and twenty quid, with twelve years of lease to run. He wearied the agent with his persistence till he succeeded in knocking off forty quid. That was a little triumph. The houses must be a bargain at three-eighty.

No sooner was the sale completed, than Bates began inquiring about for someone to give him a mortgage on the houses. It should have warned him when, at long last, he found someone willing to advance seventy pounds — only. But Bates, dazzled with all the fascinating legal procedure, disregarded that pointer. Seventy pounds was still a lot of money to him. Enough for what he had in mind next.

For naturally what he wanted was to find himself another rich bride. But she should be *rich* this time. Not like the gross fool he had just abandoned. This time he would find someone with an *income*, to whom he could fasten himself and cling forever.

To find a rich bride one had obviously to go where rich people were. Some exotic winter resort, for instance. Like Bournemouth. He would treat himself to a really posh hotel.

The grotesque *chinoiserie* of the Pine-cliff Carlton attracted him with its Freudian skyline and birthday-cake façade; he admired its baize lawns sliced with gamboge paths and punctuated every few yards with urns full of geraniums, and the winter gardens like a great glass wen bulging to one side and flashing in the sun. This last monstrosity was a steel structure jutting over the edge of the cliff and known as the Hanging Gardens.

Inside, the hideous magnificence overawed him. All that French Empire gilt and heavy druggets into which the feet sank as into quicksand, all the glass and blood-dark mahogany subdued the 'outsider' as it was meant to. The women in their furs and jewels, and their men, hard-faced and confident, almost made Bates turn and run. Even his absurd vanity could not suppose he was a match for them. For the space of perhaps sixty seconds the clerk in Reception ignored him, and at once Bates's nerves betrayed him; he was filled with rage at this insult. He was on the verge of making a hopeless exhibition of himself, when the clerk suavely attended.

They allowed him a mean little room on the top floor, overlooking a dark noisy well, from which issued inarticulate cries from the troglodytes below, who spent their days and nights, it seemed, clattering tins to and fro like thunder. He was charged eight and a half guineas a week. For Bates this had all the pleasure and guilt of great sin.

To say he was ill at ease there expresses it mildly. He caught, or fancied he caught, the pageboys tittering at him. The waiters noticed contemptuously his confusions with knives and forks, his ignorance of French menu, his ill-kept hands that he tried to hide from their gaze in his lap. They openly ignored his requests, because he did not know how to address them. But worse than all these sore little pin-pricks was the solitude. No one took any notice of him. His little attempts at civil intercourse were hastily brushed away. He was so obviously unacceptable, despite his fine new clothes.

And there were no women alone. They were in groups of twos or threes or more with their men. Once he came across a woman by herself in the lounge and affably seated himself beside her. Her eyebrows rose into her hair and she smiled oh, so frigidly. It seemed she was waiting for her husband!

He moved in restless despair from the Lounge to the Hanging Gardens and from there to the deserted Ballroom — or the Writing Room, or the Bar . . . He felt as if he was sweating out his guts.

The morning of the fourth day someone actually came across and spoke to him. A tall man with an unwieldy body he carried awkwardly, and a podgy face that perpetually wore the silly good-tempered smile one sees so often on the face of murderers in the public prints.

'May I sit down?' he said. And did so, with an air of exhaustion. His voice was hoarse, rather breathy. He smiled at Bates a bit shyly and ran long flaccid fingers through his flattened curls. 'Is it too early for a drink?'

'Not for me,' said Bates, holding up a hand. 'Thanks all the same.'

'*Quite* right,' said the stranger. '*I* won't either.' And at once looked out of all proportion depressed.

'Oh, I don't; that's all I mean. Never touch it.'

'Oh, I don't either,' he said hastily. 'But

86

this is such a *hole*, I thought it might cheer us up. I've been watching you, yesterday and today, and I've seen how depressed and jittery you were. Biting your fingers to the bone. That's why I came over. If you don't mind my *saying* so. My name's Weatherbee, by the by. Very pleased to meet you. Now, we *ought* to have something to celebrate, don't you think?'

'Don't let me stop you, please, Mr. Weatherbee.'

'No, no, I dare say I am better without it,' he said squirming his body uneasily in the chair. 'Yes, this used to be quite a bright spot in the old days. I often used to pop down for a binge. Rattling good cabaret and extension-till-midnight every weekend. And now the place is like a morgue and the people stare through you as if you were a ghost. I'd have done better to stay where I was if I wanted to be cheered up. Do you know you're the first living soul I've *spoken* to since I've been here? I'm beginning to get the horrors. You know what a *state* one's in when one first comes 'out'!' He paused

87

and his eyes sidled round to Bates. 'Do you know, I think I *will* have a drink after all. I'm as nervous as a cat.'

He ordered double whiskies and when they came drank Bates's as well as his own, draining them in straight draughts — as if they were nauseous medicine. At once he brightened up, rubbed his hands together, and said to Bates in a deep, confidential voice, 'Now tell me, quite frankly — I won't be offended, you know — what do you think about me?'

'A very nice gentleman,' said Bates uneasily.

'But what passed through your *mind* when I said I'd just come 'out,' eh?' he said keenly.

'I did just wonder how long you'd been 'away,'' suggested Bates lightly, accepting the euphemism daintily.

'Oh, splendid! That's splendid!' laughed Weatherbee. 'You did wonder that. As a matter of interest, it was nine months. *This* time. I wouldn't say that to everybody, you know. But I had a reason for saying it to you. I was sure you would understand. Now, you won't be offended, will you? I had a funny notion that you might have been 'away' too.' He breathed heavily through his smile, watching him.

'Well, that was a funny notion, I grant you. I never have,' said Bates emphatically. 'I wonder what ever gave you that idea?'

'You *really* haven't?' said Weatherbee dejectedly. 'Well, I could have *sworn*, seeing you so nervous . . . It's not very often I'm wrong about that sort of thing. I can usually tell our kind at a glance.' He signaled to the Waiter rather sulkily and said, 'Same again.'

Bates was wondering what the devil this chap, this obvious gentleman could have been 'inside' for. He looked modestly down his nose, while Weatherbee disposed of the drinks quickly, as he had before.

'I'm sorry about that,' sighed Weatherbee. 'I thought we *might* have been chums. Ha, ha!'

'Ha, ha!'

'You are not afraid of me, are you?'

'*Afraid?*'

'Well, uneasy, then. People often are,

when they know.'

'Depends, I s'pose, what you was in for?' said Bates innocently.

'Oh, that,' said Weatherbee, and stared at his fingernails. 'I'll tell you about *that* some other time. Let's enjoy ourselves now and have another drink.'

Bates sat with him politely and watched him drink. It was not a very lively occupation, and when Weatherbee could not be persuaded to leave the bar and go in to luncheon, Bates tired of him and left.

Weatherbee was no longer there when Bates came out of the dining room and he did not see him again that day. When he inquired at the desk that evening, they said Mr. Weatherbee had gone out and had not returned.

He was in the bar all right the following noon, accompanied by a woman who might have been twenty-eight or thirty-eight; appearing younger or older according to her momentary expression and the way the light fell on her face. She wore a red dress of no pretensions and a short jacket over it. She had dark, rather untidy, long hair draped carelessly off her face and fastened in a knot at her neck. Her face was quite pleasant, though her eyebrows met ominously across her nose. She wore no make-up. Just now her complexion was a shade too purple, her laughter a shade too uncontrolled.

'Come and sit down, Humphreys,' said Weatherbee cheerily. 'I want you to meet Nita.' He put his hand over hers. 'My *dear* old friend, Nita, the Countess of — Coromandel,' he rolled out the words.

The Countess giggled faintly and extended a paw. Her eyes like wet caramels clung to his stickily for a moment and then withdrew their gaze as if abashed.

Bates wondered uncomfortably if she really could be a countess.

He said tentatively, 'Are you staying here, Countess?'

She said she was. She said, it was nice here, wasn't it?

'Humphreys and I don't think so,' said Weatherbee pleasantly. 'We think it stinks.'

The Countess said she thought it was very nice.

Weatherbee tickled the back of her

neck and the Countess gave a little scream of mirth.

'Now, Nita, control yourself! There is a time and place for everything. I was *merely* pulling out your collar which was tucked in at the back. I don't know who dressed you this morning, dear, but it can't have been your *maid*.'

'Oh, dear, no!' exclaimed the Countess affectedly. 'I didn't bring my maid with me this time. I just wanted to rough it. I felt like living quite simply, the way poor people do, you know.'

She smiled kindly at Bates and gave him the teeniest wink of her bold black eye. She said, 'Tell me, what does your friend do for a living?'

'Humphreys? Oh, you must get him to tell you about it some time. He's a bit of a dark horse . . . Same again, Charlie, all round!'

'Not for me,' said Bates.

'There you are!' said Weatherbee. 'Won't drink, won't smoke! Ask him what he spends all his money *on*, Nita, the stuffy old crow!'

'Well, I think Mr. Humphreys is quite

right. I expect he's got plenty of other things to spend his money on — however much he has.' She smiled sweetly, showing discolored teeth. 'This naughty old boy drinks far more than is good for him, and he's not happy unless everyone else is doing the same.'

Weatherbee said haughtily, 'Dear me, Countess, that's the first time I've heard you complain of having *too many* drinks.'

'There are more ways of killing a cat than choking it to death with whisky,' giggled the Countess behind her hand.

She was very modestly dressed for a countess, certainly; but Bates had heard somewhere that duchesses dressed like char women, so why should not countesses dress sometimes like shop-girls or whatever? She had no wedding ring on, so that would mean that she was a countess in her own right. Bates went straight down to the Public Library after luncheon to see where Coromandel was.

On his return he found Weatherbee alone, examining the geometries of the gamboge paths. The Countess, it seemed, had a headache and had gone to lie down.

'Is she really a countess?' Bates asked.

'Certainly, certainly, certainly,' said Weatherbee, as if saying it three times made it more probable. 'A Countess of some Account!'

'Only, I never met a real countess before. I wouldn't like to have said anything to offend her, you know. We don't see many countesses where I come from in Australia.' He watched Weatherbee from the corner of his eye. 'Tell her, will you, that if I seem a bit rough stuff it's because I've never had time to be anything else.'

'Too busy making money?'

'I wouldn't call myself a poor man,' he said deprecatingly.

'Nita will be delighted to hear it; I'll certainly tell her,' Weatherbee promised. 'She goes for the simple type. Mind you, she's a good girl. I'm very fond of her myself.'

'Not married, is she?'

Weatherbee's eyebrows rose. 'Quick worker, aren't you?'

Bates colored faintly.

'I only wondered if she was a countess

in her own right.'

'*Entirely* in her own right,' Weatherbee assured him.

Bates trod beside him in silence for a while and then said abruptly, 'By the way, I don't want to put my foot in it — Does she know about you?'

'About *me*? What about me?'

'About your having been 'inside.' Being old friends, she might know, or then again, you might have kept it dark.'

'It does *amuse* me,' Weatherbee said mirthlessly, 'the way you lay people talk about it. It couldn't seem more shameful to you if I'd been in *jail!*'

Bates fell into profound silence. Not having the least idea what to say, he said nothing.

Making reddish clay scars in the gravel with his heel, Weatherbee exclaimed pettishly, 'If it had been anything I was ashamed of, *would* I have mentioned it to a complete stranger?'

'You did tell me you mentioned it because you thought I'd been 'inside' too,' Bates ventured to remind him.

With an irritable frown Weatherbee

said, 'But I would point out to you that I was a voluntary patient.'

They crunched up and down beneath the mild October sun, snapping off geranium heads as they passed. It gradually unfolded that Weatherbee was a chronic habitue of mental hospitals.

'I prefer the old-fashioned word 'asylum' myself. The word doesn't frighten *me* at all; I simply regard it as an asylum from this altogether and utterly unbearable world.' He raised up his ruddy face to smile knowingly at the reddening sun. He reiterated that the word asylum was not at all unpleasant in its associations to him because if one was a voluntary patient one was obviously un-certifiable.

He announced with a kind of dotty pride that he had been in four mental hospitals in the last five years. He caught Bates's sideways glitter, and dropped his limp white hand heavily on Bates's thigh (they were seated now on one of the pretty rustic benches made of agonizingly rustic woodwork):

'My dear fellow, you have no idea how pleasant and irresponsible the life *is* in these nuthouses. I wouldn't change places with the King himself.'

One was looked after, one was waited on hand and foot, and there were endless diversions, chess tournaments, tennis tournaments, cricket matches, dances, film shows . . . always something entertaining. It was more like a club than a hotel; if one wanted to be quiet one's desire for solitude was respected, but if one was of a loquacious turn there was nearly always somebody interesting to talk to.

Bates intimated that he did not fancy talking to someone who thought he was a poached egg or Napoleon. Weatherbee looked disgusted but passed over in silence this blunder. In the vicious newspaper he favored, Bates recollected sadistic hints of strait jackets, croton oil, padded cells — all the out-of-date horrors of Pauper Asylums.

Weatherbee's laugh rang out frankly, startling the pecking birds on the lawn.

'Look at *me*,' was his answer to that superstitious old nonsense. Though, of course, the real nuts probably did get whacked into now and then. It was different for someone like himself, as sane as the next man. In fact, he was of the opinion, rather saner than most. Or, why did they all stay out in the world struggling so hard and so vainly to keep it from being blown to pieces? The boredom and drudgery of life today! Weatherbee simply could not see that it was worthwhile. All very well before the war, when one could still live not inelegantly on one's modest competence; but today, with taxation as it was, one could not even exist. Here Weatherbee held out his hands, pathetically drooping from the wrist, to show how pitifully helpless he was by nature, finding work so dreadfully uncongenial. And really, the more he saw of the world today in his occasional excursions outside, the more he was convinced of his own wisdom and essential sanity in retreating from it. His poor shriveled little income just was sufficient to provide him with the little luxuries that are necessities if one lives in an Institution.

But if it was all so ideal, Bates wondered why he had left it.

Weatherbee explained he had been

discharged. Probably to make room for some other wretch who had bravely given up the vain struggle. Meanwhile, a little holiday, a change of air, and a bloody good 'blind'; and when his money was gone and he was alcohol-petrified, his doctor would simply get him in somewhere else.

So one had to have a doctor to get one admitted?

Bates frowned. 'But if there wasn't anything wrong with you really, surely the doctor wouldn't send you to one of those places?'

Weatherbee smiled easily. 'You'd have to convince him that there *was* something wrong of course. It's not so hard when you know the trick.'

The coal-red sun slid behind a bank of cloud on the horizon and the wind off the sea blew the evening chill toward them. As they slowly climbed the steps to the hotel, Weatherbee, puffing a little, his soft hand pressing on Bates's shoulder, narrated the beginnings of the affair. It opened in the early days of the war, when His Majesty had rashly called him to the colors. In those days, Weatherbee modestly admitted, he really used to drink. And life in the Army made him drink more than ever. Perhaps he *had* been a little neurotic then, he mused. More and more of his time was spent in what they quaintly called the Glasshouse. He determined either to hook it or to crook it, but get out he would. He had studied a bit of this psycho stuff before the war and he knew the line to pull. He put on an act that the M.O. swallowed like wine. Officially he was only given a temporary discharge, pending psychiatric treatment; but whenever his case came up for review it seemed always to be at 'a critical juncture in the treatment.' Weatherbee giggled.

'You were smart,' said Bates enviously.

'Anyone could have done it if they had the brains.'

'Ah! But suppose the M.O. had been the one with the brains? Suppose he hadn't believed you?'

'My dear man, one has to make it convincing. And then, it's not like a broken leg, you know.'

'How do you mean?'

Weatherbee said loftily, 'They can't X-ray a psychosis, or discover the state of your mind through a blood-test or a urinoscopy.'

'I see,' said Bates blankly. 'Then how do they tell?'

'They ask questions, and watch you, and write down what you do and say. But if you've got your wits about you, it's all on your side; for they put the damnedest interpretations on what seem to you quite sensible replies.'

'Ah, you knew what to say.'

'I'd read it up, that's all. Anyone could do it who could read words of ten syllables.'

'Well, what are you boys looking so gloomy about?' said the Countess brightly, sitting down between them in her crumpled red frock.

7

I Like a Man to Have Nice Feelings

The night Weatherbee passed out, the Countess wandered downstairs and said to Bates, 'The poor old chap isn't feeling too grand, so I made him go to bed.' She put her little head archly on one side, 'Oh dear, shan't I be blue all on my ownio tonight!'

So they dined together. Bates was afraid she would want a lot to drink, but she kept her demands modest, and she was unusually serious and sympathetic: she wanted to hear all about Humphreys' life in Australia. His reserve only seemed natural. Once she pressed his foot under the table. Bates was bloated with conceit of himself: a countess was no different from any other bag after all. It was going to be a cinch.

She gave him a coy look (he was very heavy going), 'I'm rather glad poor old

Weatherbee passed out; gave us a chance to get to know each other.'

'So he passed out, did he? I thought so.'

'Pardon my slip!' said the Countess, with a hand over her mouth to stifle a giggle. 'I didn't mean to give the poor old chap away.'

'Oh, I know all about him; he's told me.'

The Countess looked faintly puzzled, but did not pursue it.

Groping in her bag, her cockscomb hands with their bitten fingernails brought out a crumpled handkerchief, a grubby puff, a roll of notes, and a comb, tumbling them on the cloth till she found the broken package of cigarettes she was looking for. The sight of those notes stirred Bates like love; he hardly knew how to keep his hands off them; his nostrils dilated and his breathing quickened, and the hunger with which he gazed at the Countess resembled passion.

He did not know the best way to woo a countess, but decided that flowers would make a good effect. He bought her a dozen red roses the next day. The price was scandalous — for *flowers!* It made the blood beat up into his thin cheeks. So much money for something so ephemeral. Even after he had presented them, he could not take his eyes off them. It seemed to him she did not sufficiently appreciate them. He kept staring at their burning red beauty, licking his dry lips.

'Looking at my flowers?' said the Countess archly. 'Pretty, aren't they?'

'I like them,' he said weakly.

'I can see you do. And I like you for it. I like a man to have nice feelings,' she smiled.

The next day Weatherbee was with them again, but a shaky old Weatherbee who could hardly lift a glass to his lips without spilling it. He looked better when he had had a few drinks to pull him together.

'Have you pinched my girlfriend, while I've been away, Humphreys? I did think I could trust *you*.'

'Oh, Georgie, these Australians are terrible,' said the Countess.

'I haven't actually *pinched* her yet,' said Bates deprecatingly, with a sideways glance, 'but I have given her a bit of a squeeze now and again.'

The Countess giggled wildly behind her hand at this piece of wit, and Bates was elated with his success.

But later that same day she came to him, her face flushed beneath a careless flurry of powder. Her left eye was purple to the cheekbone. Her nose looked swollen. She directed him tersely to follow, her, and she took him to a distant corner of the deserted Hanging Gardens. Rain lashed the glass walls and they could see the sea heaving sullenly below them. The draft piercing through the steel frames rustled the potted palms in an incessant irritating whisper.

Without the least warning the Countess thrust herself at him and burst into angry sobs. 'Oh, my God!' she said. 'Oh, my God, Mr. Humphreys!'

'Countess, whatever's the matter? You're trembling!'

'That brute! That filthy brute!' She pressed his hand to her bosom. 'Feel how my heart's beating!' she said.

It emerged between incoherence and

tears that Weatherbee had forced his way into her room on some pretext and had then apparently gone quite mad and 'assaulted' her.

What was so shocking was that they had been friends for years (just friends, nothing in it, dear!) and now she felt she couldn't bear ever to see him again. She was shattered. She wanted dear Mr. Humphreys to be a true friend and help her to get away at once.

Bates's heart leaped, but he only pressed her hand cautiously.

'The point is this,' she said, 'the banks are all shut now, and I've got to pay my bill here and that rotter's too. You see, it was my idea to do him a good turn, being an old friend as I told you, and I invited him here for a little spree. I thought it would do him good. And my own place is being done up just now. (Maltravers Towers. I hope you'll come and visit me there. I'd go there now if only the place wasn't chockablock with workmen.) Still, so long as we can go right away from here — I just don't feel I can see George again. The only problem is about the money. I invited him here for three weeks.'

'Well, I don't see you need bother about that after the way he's treated you.'

'I don't feel I can let him down, he's not very well off, you know. Of course I could leave him a check, but he might tear that up to spite me. What I want is to leave him notes; no one can ever resist notes. It'd be such a smack in the eye for him to find fifty quid in an envelope.'

'I wouldn't mind a smack in the eye like that,' laughed Bates.

'Ah, but you're different, Humphie dear. That swine George is going to feel damned humiliated when he sees that money and knows he's here on my purse and he hasn't even been able to behave himself properly. He'll feel a fool. And that's what I want him to feel. I want to insult him, the dirty brute!' She leaned toward him and cast down her eyes shyly. 'Humphie,' she murmured, 'could you be a dear and lend me the money — just till tomorrow, when I can go to the bank. I don't know what you must think of me asking you like this, and I couldn't if I didn't need it so badly.' Seeing him hesitate, she said hastily, 'Of course I'll give you security — '

'It wasn't that. I just was thinking of all that money you had on you last night — pardon my mentioning it! — but I should have thought there was enough there for what you wanted.'

'Oh, no, my dear, not nearly. Not more than thirty quid or so, and I shall have to have something for tipping and fares. But I can give you my jewels as security. I wouldn't like you to feel you were being forced into anything. My pearls alone are worth three hundred, and I only want to borrow fifty quid or so.' She watched him astutely.

He said uncomfortably, 'Of course I don't want any security from you, Countess. It isn't that.'

Poor Bates had never been in such a predicament. He had never needed to invent for himself the rule never to lend money — as though he would ever have parted with it, even if he had had it to lend! Yet this occasion was so different. If he refused he might lose her. He wanted to tell her he hadn't that much cash on him, hut she rallied him sharply, 'Oh, come on, what's fifty quid to you! I hope you're not mean, Humphreys. I can't stand mean men.' There seemed nothing else for it then.

When at last he handed it over, she kissed him impulsively in full view of whoever. 'You're a sweetie!' she said.

He saw her hand the envelope with the notes in to the Reception to be given to Mr. Weatherbee.

'I'll just pack my things and meet you in the lounge in half an hour,' she told Bates, giving him the old glad-eye. As the lift swept her out of sight, she blew him a kiss . . . the last he saw of the Countess.

It would be too painful to describe the slow discovery of his loss. He never forgot how the clerk's face reddened with suppressed laughter when he asked for the Countess of Coromandel's room number. By that time she was lost in the back streets of Bournemouth.

He ran in a rage to Weatherbee, whom he found lying in his bed, staring at the changing sky through an inch of greenish liquid at the bottom of a glass he was holding to the light.

'Where's my money? You hand it over or I'll send for the police!' he threatened.

But at that instant he saw the envelope lying unopened beside the siphon, and he snatched it up and tore it open. Inside was a folded wad of lavatory paper.

Weatherbee swilled down the last of his drink and swung off the bed to get some more. Bates managed to stutter out a few explanatory, expostulatory phrases.

Weatherbee began to laugh helplessly, his cheeks shaking. Excess of mirth poured in tears down his face. Every fresh glance at Bates's glowering face sent him off afresh, speechlessly. He writhed. He was in agony. He had to lie flat on his back on the floor to recover. But once he had exhausted his amusement, he sat up as solemn as a funeral mute without even the ability left to smile.

He had been pulling Humphreys' leg of course — meaning no harm by it: Nita was just a girl he had picked up in a bar downtown, just one of the girls. He had brought her back to liven up his lonely nights and days, because he liked to have a drinking companion and she had seemed a good sort. There was no one better than a lousy old 'professional' if you wanted a tolerant and good-humored companion. He had trusted her with his money even, so that he should not do anything foolish with it when he was out of this world.

But when he rejoined them after his little disappearance, it seemed to him that Nita was playing Humphreys on the side and just using himself as a meal ticket. So he had it out with her. Where whores were concerned, his motto was always: Where you sleep must pay your keep. He hadn't the least objection in the world to her trying to make Humphreys because he was a wealthier man, he quite understood a girl had to live; but he didn't intend to pay for Humphreys' entertainments. That was only fair. So he dug the money out of her that she was minding for him, and told her to clear.

You'd never have thought she had such a temper. She raised the devil! Threw an inkstand at him (here Bates noticed for the first time the blue rivulets on the painted door), kicked a lump out of his shin and damned nearly gouged one of his ears off. Then the management had come up to complain, and she had slammed out.

It was after that that she had sobbed on Bates's shoulder and spun her tale.

Bates 'borrowed' from Weatherbee the money to pay his bill and see him back to town. But the experience was a shock to him — his overpowering self-confidence was suddenly undermined. Perhaps it was this that caused him to lose his judgment.

8

There's Someone in the Chimbley

In London, he pawned his peacock's feathers and found a squalid room for himself, and scowling went out to bully his wretched tenants and chivvy them into paying their arrears of rent. With this and with that, he raised enough cash to cover the premium on a fire insurance policy on his bit of property.

And then by one of those coincidences only the hardiest or the stupidest would attempt to bring off, barely a fortnight later, some faulty wiring short-circuited and the buildings were burned to the ground. The luckless tenants escaped with their lives in their ragged night-clothes. Whatever meager treasures they possessed were gone forever. Destitute, homeless, they stood in the streets, shivering and watching the flames lick away all they owned.

Bates applied at once for the insurance, but a series of maddening and unreasonable delays occurred. The Company seemed not entirely satisfied, though Bates was able to assure them that he had not visited the place since he took out his policy. Possibly that crude assurance only strengthened their suspicions. At any rate, the money was not forthcoming. The little job had been performed in vain. And in addition the ground-landlord promised to sue him for the difference between the insurance-cover and the cost of rebuilding: an impossible amount.

Bates was rattled. God, who wouldn't be? Now he was down the drain! He had *lost* nearly four hundred quid — not counting the sour little episode with the 'Countess,' and now as well had the threat of some fiendish lawyer chasing him with a writ. He panicked for an idea with which to save himself. Sought some way still to give himself the luxury he craved and so richly reserved.

At this nadir the recollection of Weatherbee prompted him to a new endeavor. (Every man by his actions chooses the death he is to die.) The thought of the pleasant idle life Weather-bee had described haunted him with longing. He was seized by an over whelming desire to be his undisguised self for once, and there it would be only natural for him to express his ferocious envy and hatred of life openly. The notion began to seduce him. He took pains to study the case-histories in the heavy medical tomes in the Free Library. He was not so stupid that he could not piece together some sort of pattern of behavior.

When he felt ready, he made them send for the doctor in the middle of the night. 'I won't, I tell you! I won't,' he kept calling out, disturbing the other inmates of the dingy lodging house, so that they banged on ceiling and wall for quiet, till the whole building racketed with cries and blows.

Bates greeted the doctor coolly, taking aback that gaunt, nerve-driven man, who expected in that quarter of London to see someone an hour from death, and not a man, white-faced, it is true, and hair on end, but otherwise in perfect health.

'What have you called me out for?' he said, sharp with fatigue.

Bates put a finger to his lips. 'Hush! Do you hear him?' he whispered, pointing to the rusty broken fireplace. 'There's someone in the chimbley,' he explained, 'and he keeps telling me to kill myself. Soon as I drop off to sleep, he starts up. 'Go on!' he says. Listen! 'Go on, cut your throat!' Can you hear him?'

That was a splendid beginning, but Bates required to go carefully if he was to be a voluntary patient and not a certified lunatic.

In the light of day, in the doctor's shabby surgery, he had to be quieter, vaguer altogether. The doctor looked at the inside of his eyelids, inquired if his stools were regular, and gave him a bottle of bromide.

Bates's point was that he wanted to be prevented from killing himself. He was afraid that one day the 'voice' would drive him to it. He said frankly that his object was to get shut away somewhere where he couldn't do himself any harm.

The doctor soon got sick of being

dragged out at all hours, and sent him to one of the free London clinics for the treatment of nervous diseases.

The psychiatrist who took charge of Bates (alias Leonard Hardy this time) was a frail young man with horned spectacles and a gentle manner that seemed to verge on timidity. He had lost his right arm in the war. Although his patients, through ignorance or a desire to be civil, called him doctor he had no right to the title. He was really a lay psychiatrist, and hoped in time to take his degree.

Yet he was altogether a different proposition from the G.P. He vouchsafed nothing but listened without comment to what Bates had to tell him. This made it difficult for Bates to tell whether his story was going over properly, and gave him no hint what he should 'put in' or 'take out.'

There were several things about this queer little cockney that puzzled Mr. Titmuss, the psychiatrist. Something did not seem quite to hang together. The delusions were typically schizophrenic; what was not so typical was Hardy's extra delusory behavior. Unlike most patients suffering from this disorder, he seemed incapable of speaking the truth about himself. It was impossible to get at his past history in sequence. He shrank from close questioning, eluded inquiry.

Bates never knew quite how dotty he should appear to be, and was mortally afraid of giving himself away. He could blurt out the brief sentences which served to describe his imaginary past in Australia, but he was incapable of flowing out a stream of invention; he dreaded this analysis the doctor was so keen on.

He could not persuade the doctor to get him safely put away. In fact he was rather worse off than he had been before, because he could not harry this doctor or call him out in the middle of the night — a bare hour three times a week was all he got, and it was getting him nowhere. It could not go on like this. He determined to force the issue. And having found out where the doctor lived he went round there late one night and made a scene.

It was like some crude old woodcut, the two of them struggling on that ill-lit staircase, the one-armed man leaning against the banisters and the other brandishing an open razor that flashed in the yellow gloom.

Titmuss' flat was at the top of this old Victorian house. He was sweating; a man with only one arm is at a terrible disadvantage against a madman with both arms and a razor. With all the authority he could command he ordered Hardy to behave himself.

'If you shut the door on me now,' shouted Bates, 'I swear I'll cut me bloody throat on your staircase.'

Eventually Titmuss got him into the sitting room, where he collapsed dramatically, dropping like a stone into the depths of a springless sofa.

'Cry if you want to,' Titmuss said. 'It'll make you feel better.' He pottered from the room — it was quite safe to leave him now his hysteria had subsided — to make the man a cup of tea. He was back in less than five minutes with the tea, standing over the prostrate man, saying, 'Come, Mr. Hardy! Sit up and drink this. Then you can go home.'

Bates sat up sullenly and without

looking at him said, 'I got no home. I got no money, and nowhere to go. I'm desprit. I keep telling you I'm desprit and you don't take no notice. What am I to do? Foxes got holes and birds of the air got nests, but here's the son of man without anywhere to lay his head!' he cried accusingly with the powerful wail of a street preacher, enraged that the man should be making it so hard for him.

'What do you want me to do?' asked Mr. Titmuss, with deceptive simplicity.

'I keep telling you, don't I? I want you to get me in somewhere I'll be looked after, somewhere I can't do myself no harm. I'm scared I'll do myself an injury. I get scared to pick up a knife or do anything, with these voices of mine always on at me. And it's getting worse. Besides which I'm worried to death not having anywhere to go and no means of earning a livelihood. Sometimes looks to me it would be best all round if I did do for myself. Only it seems like I never had a chance to live proper,' he whined. 'If I got properly looked after for a few months . . . '

The man was only interested in getting his own way, and he would not believe that Titmuss was not in a position to qualify him for a mental hospital. Still, the man was in a wretched state and if penniless could hardly be turned out of doors at this time of night. Mr. Titmuss said he might bed down there. Just for the night.

That was Mr. Titmuss' fatal mistake. Having once taken him in he found it impossible to get rid of him. It seemed so long as Hardy could attach himself parasitically to somebody, he was content. He was like a leech, clinging irremovably; or even more like a tick, burrowing in the flesh, only to be dug out with a knife. And Titmuss' weakness was a dread of scenes — of his own making; he put off from day to day the ultimate struggle, because he could not afford for it to happen unless he was the victor. And he was not sure of his strength against this doleful, white-faced wretch always complaining and watching at the edge of his eyes.

Mr. Titmuss had suggested that by way of earning his keep Hardy should do the housework as a form of occupational therapy, but his notions of housework proved lamentably sketchy. If at least he had been useful to Titmuss, the outcome might have been different.

Titmuss began to miss little things, trifles like handkerchiefs and socks and small coins. The whole affair was becoming tedious and irritating. It was not even as if Hardy was a pleasant character; it was simply that too weak to dig, he was not ashamed to beg; and however often Titmuss told him he must be gone by nightfall, he was always still to be found skulking there on his return.

Bates had dug himself in very comfortably. It was a convenient irresponsible life, almost idle enough; and from his private studies among the doctor's papers during his absence, he believed he had acquired enough information to keep the doctor under his thumb should he turn awkward. He was cautiously holding that knowledge for the right moment.

It came sooner than he expected.

One Wednesday evening Mr. Titmuss pushed away his dinner of cold corned beef and raw tomatoes and announced that Hardy would have to make other arrangements after Saturday, because he had accepted an appointment in Johannesburg and was leaving by plane for South Africa on Saturday. He casually displayed the ticket.

Hardy spluttered with indignation at being 'let down' so coolly, and when Titmuss was not moved, began to whine. And when Titmuss was not moved, began to threaten.

That was a mistake. Titmuss, though weak, was not to be blackmailed. He countered with a warning about the police and Hardy rashly laughed — holding all the cards. Or so he thought.

At length, Titmuss naturally not wishing his arrangements to be delayed through tiresomeness with the police, said, 'I'll give you a few hours to think it over, before I send for the police. I think tomorrow you may feel differently.'

Bates said nothing, with evil effect, and slammed into his room. He could hardly breathe for rage. Anger boiled in his breast so that it rose like a choking phlegm into his throat. The brass candlestick, the bright metallic surface of the mirror, the lampstand, all became dark and menacing, shifting jerkily as he turned his eyes from one to the other. He pressed his fingers to his eyeballs in terror; alarmed by the darkening world, and the fix he had got himself into. Titmuss seemed to him now just the sort of squealing weakling who would go to the police. He'd have to stop that, if it was the last thing he did. (Or if it was the last thing Titmuss did, flashed malevolently into his teeming brain, but he shuddered away from it — he had a superstitious horror of violence.)

He had notions of 'skipping' there and then, before harm could come to him, but swore he wouldn't leave penniless. Yet there was danger there too; Titmuss was not a man who collected about him evidences of his taste and wealth, in short there were no little costly objects in the flat that could be easily picked up and stowed away, nor did he keep large sums of money about him; in fact, the only valuable Bates could think of was the ticket to South Africa. If he could get his hands on that in time for the airline company to refund a cancellation at full value, he would do well. But the danger was that even if he managed to get hold of it and 'skip,' Titmuss might quite well discover its loss before the airline opened in the morning and he would warn them before Bates could get there. (Then Titmuss must be *prevented* from discovering the theft. Or, having discovered it, from complaining about it. If somehow that could be done! Bates's mind besought him to consider it, but still he blinked away from it. There must be some other, some safer way.)

He paced up and down the slip of space between his bed and the chest of drawers. If Titmuss should die in the night . . . If he should fall in the bath and break his neck. Alas, accidents were not arranged to benefit a third party! *Unless . . . accidents were 'arranged!'*

His face, a white patch in the dark mirror, looked strangely back at him. In an orgasm of self-pity he burst into sobs. 'God, what are they driving me to?' he moaned, sinking on to his knees and folding his arms above his head. 'It's not my fault, if they won't let me live in peace, with their threats!' All night he whimpered and plotted, like a reluctant schoolboy; yet morning found him as impassive as usual.

9

Murder on the Brain

His manner was very subdued when he went to call Mr. Titmuss.

'I'm sorry about last night, sir; I don't know what came over me,' he said, his inflamed lids meek in his haggard face.

Titmuss gave him a look so crisply sardonic that Bates's heart plunged in fear of his pre-knowledge.

'I'll run your bath, sir,' he said quickly and was still fidgeting about the bathroom when Titmuss came in.

'All right. Clear out now.'

'Yes, sir. I'm just going out for half a minute, Mr. Titmuss,' he said meekly. 'I'll bring the phone in. If it rings while I'm out it'll save you getting out of the bath. I'm only going out to get something for your breakfast, sir; it slipped my mind yesterday.'

'Don't trouble,' said Titmuss, loosening

the cord of his dressing gown, contemptuously amused by Hardy's belated
deference.

'No trouble, sir,' Bates assured him,
carefully arranging the phone on a stool
at the right hand of the left-handed man.
With the bath full as it was now it would
be difficult for a one-armed man using
the phone to prevent the flex trailing into
the water.

Bates heard the door locked against
him and ran out of the flat and down the
stairs. It was from now on all a question
of timing.

The grocer was raising his iron shutters
with a rattle of thunder, as Bates ran past.
Some two hundred yards away at the
corner of the street stood a telephone
booth. Toward this Bates scurried, till he
saw that the glass was darkened by a
figure within.

Bates stood helplessly in the windswept
street, petrified by this unexpected error
in his calculations. What was he to do? He
had counted on the phone box not being
in use at this hour of the morning. He
had no notion where the next nearest one

was. He could not think where to go, what to try; he was bounced by the idea that already it might be too late, that Titmuss might even now be ringing the police.

The woman in the box looked carelessly right into his terrified eyes and laughed down the phone; Bates quickly put his hand over his face, so that at least she should not have time to memorize the features. He moved round and leaned his back against the door, till she pushed against it to come out.

'Sorry to have kept you waiting,' she said brightly as she passed, but he kept his head down and scuttled into the box. His fingers were so slippery he could hardly push the pennies into the slot. He dialed; heard Titmuss say, 'Hello'; and pressed Button A.

'Hullo,' Titmuss kept saying querulously. 'Who is it?'

But all his prepared intentions had slipped from Bates's mind in the confusion of the last few minutes.

'It's me,' he said faintly at last.

'What's that? Speak up, I can't hear

you. Who's 'me'?'

'Bates,' he said loudly. And in a sudden panic lest Titmuss should lose patience or take it for some practical joke, Bates brought down the mouthpiece of the receiver against the metal coin box with all his strength. There was an appalling ringing sound that vibrated outward like a stone in a pond . . . and another less definable sound. And when Bates put the receiver to his ear again there was only the long empty silence of a dead line . . .

Well, now it was over. Bates marched stiffly back up the street and turned in at the grocer's. He blinked about him dazedly, tried to remember why he had come in here, and did remember.

'Bloaters?' he asked.

'No bloaters,' said the grocer curtly.

This small setback upset him disproportionately. The decision to ask for bloaters had risen automatically from his memory; now his mind was quite a blank and he could not think of a single item to ask for instead. He stood there stupidly, looking about him but seeing nothing.

'Nice tinner sardines?' suggested the

grocer, turning to the shelves behind him. 'Portuguese,' he said holding them out indifferently.

Bates was on the point of saying that would do, when the recollection flashed to his mind that there were already two tins of sardines in the larder. It startled him like a piece of ice dropped down his back. What a blunder if, in answer to the question he expected to come later, he had said he had gone out to buy sardines for the doctor's breakfast, when there were already some in the house.

'I'll have a quarter of breakfast sausage,' he choked out hurriedly.

'You don't look too good, Mr. 'ardy,' said the grocer sociably, his eyes on the scales.

'Toothache,' mumbled Bates, paling.

'Oh, that's a shocking awful thing! One and twopence 'apenny. Don't know what we got teeth for at all. Nothing but a nuisance from the start, are they?'

'That's right,' fidgeted Bates. 'Don't bother about that. I gotter get back. Left my gentleman in his bath and if I don't give him his breakfast in time, he'll be late, and that'll mean trouble all round . . .'

He ran across the road, the thin package swinging from his finger . . .

He was gone less than five minutes. The grocer glanced up at the clock, and back at the figure in the doorway, exclaiming in alarm, 'Oh, Mr. 'ardy, whatever's the matter?'

Bates came into the shop with the curious stilted step of a crane. He said stiffly, 'Mr. Fennel, I'd be obliged if you'd come back with me a minute. There's been an accident. He's dead. I think he's dead. He doesn't answer, and he's locked in the bathroom. It muster happened while I was out, you see!'

Mr. Fennel left his wife in charge of the shop, and accompanied Mr. Hardy across the road.

They broke open the bathroom door without much difficulty.

'Poor young man!'

He had his story pat, and there was Fennel to confirm it for him. The police did not make a long-drawn affair of it. It seemed a straightforward enough case of misadventure. Most people knew the dangers of telephoning in the bath; for a one-armed man it was foolhardy in the extreme. If such a person made a habit of it, he was sure sooner or later to fall foul of the wires.

The police checked the phone call, but as it turned out to be from a phone booth that proved a dead end. They found out about Titmuss' contract with the South African people naturally; but they were hardly to suppose he had already bought his ticket since they did not find it among his effects. They disliked the servant's mien, he had an untrustworthy appearance, there hung about him the indescribable odor of the petty criminal; but even a policeman cannot go on suspicion alone and there was nothing to suggest he had any connection with the misadventure. They were a little rough to him, and he was insolently bland in return.

In fact he was rather pleased with himself. It had all been so easy. In due course he collected the money from the airline company, and disappeared.

Mr. Fennel could have told the police a bit more. He would have liked to rid himself of some of the queer things that puzzled him. He had to give evidence at the inquest, but despite the oath to tell the truth, the whole truth, and nothing but the truth, Fennel found it is not possible to tell the *whole* truth unless one is asked all the questions.

One of the things he wondered about at night, watching the lamplight on the ceiling, was where Hardy had been hurrying to that morning before he came into the shop the first time. He had seen Hardy's reflection in the plate-glass window as he was lifting the shutters. It must have been seven or eight minutes later that he entered the shop.

'You can't even be sure it was 'im,' said his wife impatiently. 'Not sure enough to swear to it. You couldn't have seen more than a grayish sort of shadow in the glass, if you 'ad your back to him.'

'It was him all right,' said Fennel.

Oh, men! The stubborn things! thought Lil Fennel with angry tenderness, watching her Morrie lying there worrying, with his nose poking up toward the ceiling. Why couldn't they ever leave things alone, same as women did? Nice state the world would be in if women went round fussing over a lot of muddles no one couldn't put straight.

'He might've gone to the tobacconist's,' she said helpfully.

'What for?' her Morrie said wearily. 'He don't smoke and I 'appen to know his gentleman smoked a pipe.'

'Well, then, he went to the phone booth; and what does that prove?'

'It don't prove a thing. Don't I wish it did. But, you must say, Lil, it's *rum* that this poor sick chap was killed by a call that came from a phone booth just at the very identical time 'ardy was out of the house and *could* of been telephoning from that box down the road. What I wonder is, why the police never asked if he'd been seen by anyone down there?'

'Wish you'd give it a rest and wonder yourself to sleep.'

'You go to sleep, then, no one's stopping you. I'll just lie here quiet and try and puzzle it out.'

Lil sighed. 'Can't you see: even if he was seen telephoning it still don't prove anything. He might have been phoning a friend . . . I don't see why you're so keen to make out he murdered the poor chap. I should have thought if that was what he was after he'd have done best to drop the phone in the bath and walk out — at least that way he'd know he was dead for sure.'

'Walk out and leave the bathroom door locked on the inside. That's clever, I must say. How would he do that?'

'They do it in detective stories,' said his wife vaguely.

'This isn't a detective story; this is real life,' he said irritably. There was a pause while Fennel remembered how haggard and gray the man had looked that morning, and how sprightly he had been later — offensively so, Fennel had thought at the time. Not at all flustered either, seemed to know just what he had to do. It hadn't been natural, say what you like.

'Do let's get some sleep, Morrie Fennel, can't we?' cried Lil, flumping round in bed.

'You can't just do nothing, Lil, if you think there's been a murder done.'

136

'You'll give yourself murder on the brain if you don't give it a rest,' she scolded, and then coaxingly, stretching out her warm arms to him, 'Come here, you old silly, you.'

But the comfort of his Lil's embrace did not last long. Shamefaced but conscientious, he went at last to the police.

10

Hoping That Fate Will Not Part Us Long

This 'windfall' from Dennis Titmuss, Bates invested in a roadside snackbar. God knows what fantasy led him to suppose that he could make a success of it! His idea was to make a quick turnover and sell out at a profit. Yes, for he would never keep working for long. *That* was not his line at all. Meanwhile it was a pleasure to be fingering money all day.

There was a little woman who used to come in regularly for coffee and a bun. She always read while she ate. A sallow drab little woman in her fifties, the manageress of a cleaning establishment up the street. Bates noticed her because of the brooch that sparkled at her throat. Sometimes small earrings flashed as she turned her head.

He kept an eye on her as an interesting

proposition. The business was doing badly under his inexpert management but he could still appear a man of substance to her. He found out how she kept her money, her savings; he was always irresistible on that tack, women poured out their financial secrets to him as if he were their broker or their bank manager.

Annie Grun her name was. Her father had been German. After the First World War and her mother's death, her father took her back to his fatherland. 'This will be the life, Annie, you will see,' he had told her. (She caught glimpses through plate-glass windows of a wild lubricous carnival, whose hysteria reeked of death rather than life.)

All her life long she remembered the casual sight of terror or despair on the faces of strangers passing in the street. *Inflation!* Her father coming into her room that day with a face like wax. The notes fluttering and falling out of his hands. And when she knelt to gather them up, he said in a queer hard voice, as if the words were being ground out of his throat by a little mill, 'Don't trouble,

Annie. They are not worth picking up.'

She remembered him trailing over to the window.

'Papa, are you sick?' she had called.

All her life she was to remember how slowly the windows burst open beneath his weight, how slowly he seemed to fall . . .

Inflation!

She understood about that later. She learned not to trust banks or stocks and shares — that was what they could do to you. For the rest of her barren little life her aim was always to turn her earnings into something solid as quickly as she could, something that had intrinsic value. She disliked holding paper money even for a short while. Paper money wasn't real and its value could melt like snow overnight — she knew. Year by year her savings were converted into trinkets of diamond or gold. That was safe. She knew.

Yet all her caution, all her suspiciousness, availed her little against the flashy authority of Thomas Bates. In no time she was sidling into a registry office on his arm, to emerge as Mrs. Marsh. She had a fancy for Selsey for her honeymoon, and — her Johnny infinitely tolerant of female whims — that was where they went.

On the morning of their second day in Selsey, strolling in the pale sunshine arm in arm, Bates conscientiously breathing deep gusts of ozone (a pity to waste fresh air if you had to pay for it), his busy inquisitive eye remarked a woman in a fur coat gazing into a dress-shop window. It was the fur coat that attracted his notice in the first place. On this bland spring morning this was the only fur coat in Selsey High Street, so he gave it a second glance and saw that the shape it took, something about the way it hung from the shoulders, was odiously familiar. The handbag swinging by its handle, the velvet picture hat; yes, it was undoubtedly that girl, Grace Pickering. She must have come into money!

A bird in the hand was never worth two in the bush to Bates; his design was always to have all *three*. If he did not at least find out what Grace was up to here and how she came to be sporting such a handsome fur coat, his business conscience would give him no peace.

He halted. (Every man by his actions chooses the death he is to die.) And said briskly to his new wife, 'Excuse me half a tick, Annie. I seen someone I used to know. An old friend. You walk on, if you like.'

She gave him a quick, offended look and moved apart.

Grace was turning from the window. He went up to her, smiling.

'Hullo, Grace!' he said, raising his hat like a gentleman.

The color drained slowly out of her cheeks leaving them a dirty yellow. Her eyes showed the white all round. You could tell it had given her a shock.

She pulled her dry lips apart to whisper, '*Freddy!*'

'What are you doing here all on your own and looking so smart?' he said saucily.

At this cool attack, the color flooded back into her face angry red.

'Well, you've got a nerve, I must say. I don't know how you dare come up and

142

speak to me, after all these months without a word!' she spluttered, but he cut in airily:

'It's no good throwing a fit about it. I can explain everything, but I'm not going into it now, there isn't time. You gotter trust me, Grace. Have I ever lied to you? Have I ever broken my word?'

'You said you'd write.'

'I did write. Again and again. If you never got the letters, ask yer dad what happened to them, but don't blame me.'

'Daddy wouldn't do such a thing; he's honorable!' she cried angrily, but Freddy remained unperturbed.

'Okay! If you'd sooner believe your father than your own husband . . . ' He smiled briefly, his crooked mirthless smile, and raised his hat again.

She had forgotten how frighteningly easily he became offended. She called after him, 'Why didn't you come down to see me, then, when I never answered your letters?'

He turned. Shrugged.

'I did. But what's the use of telling you if you're determined to take your father's

143

word against mine — even though you know he was dead against me from the first . . . He said you didn't live there anymore; he said you'd gone away.' He gave a little, dry, expressionless laugh, 'And to think of the money I spent hunting for you all over, only to get a raspberry when at last I find you!'

'Were you down here looking for *me?*'

'Well, what yer think I'm doing in this dead end, neglecting my work and everything?'

'Oh, Freddy!' Her tears came up easily. 'I'm so sorry. I've been so unhappy, so worried. You don't know how I've missed you. And everyone said . . . '

'Oh, yes, I bet everyone *said!* Now, buck up, Grace, do! They're all looking at you. You can't cry in the street! Here!' He pushed her up a quiet alley, where there was no one to notice them but a woman so fat she looked as if she was wedged in the open window.

'You haven't told me yet what *you're* doing here? And looking so smart, too,' he repeated. 'Someone left you a fortune?'

'Only poor Granny; she died last

January. But Freddy,' Grace said hurriedly, guiltily, determined to get it off her chest straight away so that there should be no deception, 'Freddy, she left me the money all tied up so even *I* can't touch it. All I get is the income, see?'

'She left you a big sum, then,' he remarked softly. 'You still haven't told me why you're here and where you're staying.'

'Oh, I'm just having a little holiday, staying with friends. They've got a ducky little bungalow on the beach. You must meet them, dear,' she said hesitantly.

'You bet I will. Got to thank 'em for looking after my wife for me, before I take her away. Now that I've found her, she needn't think I'm going to let her out of my sight again in a hurry.' He preened like a bantam.

Grace was quite overcome at the implications of this loving speech, and threw herself on his breast, tipping her hat awry.

'Oh, Freddy! Freddy, darling! You haven't even kissed me yet.'

'I'm not going to either, with that great

cow watching and grinning all over her mug. Street's not the place for kissing, anyway. Plenty of time later for kissing and canoodling,' he said with ferocious bonhomie, giving her a friendly *nip* that made her squeal.

The squeal led to another squeal when she saw the time.

'Oh, dear! It's nearly lunchtime. I don't know . . . I hardly like . . . What do you think I ought to do, Freddy?'

'You run along to your dinner, that's all right. Don't bother about me. I got plenty to see to. It wouldn't do for me to come barging in like this, you break it to them first. Tell them I'll be round about teatime, I shouldn't wonder. Give you time to get your things together.'

'Do you want me to come away tonight? Won't that seem a bit rude to Doris and Frank, leaving in such a hurry?'

'Never mind Doris and Frank; leave them to me. They'll naturally expect you to want to be with your husband now.'

'But, darling, where are we going?'

'Anywhere in the whole wide world,

except Worthing. I wouldn't want to run into your Pa, I might do him an injury. I'm not one to easy forgive a wrong done me, Grace, my girl,' he said pompously.

'Freddy, darling! I'm afraid to let you go in case you disappear and I never see you again. You will come this afternoon, won't you? Promise me!'

'You won't lose me this time, never fear!' he grinned.

And then when he got back to the boardinghouse at five minutes past one (everyone looked away as he entered the dining room, embarrassed by his unpunctuality — one of the deadly sins) it was to find that Annie had worked herself up into a fume. She sipped her tepid soup and would not speak (he had forfeited the first course by his lateness).

He totally disregarded her ill humor, and leaned across to break off a crust of her bread to munch while he waited (no soup — no bread!).

'Sea air gives you an appetite, don't it?' he said cheerily to the dark buttoned face opposite. But it wasn't the sea air that filled him with this ravenous well-being.

God, it was a bright day, it was a lucky day at last! If ever man deserved a bit of luck, he did. Behind his impassive mask, his heart was singing. Happy as a wolf!

As soon as they were in their bedroom again, Annie shut the door grimly and said, hardly moving her tight little mouth:

'Now, understand, Johnny Marsh, you're not going to make a fool out of me!'

'Who wants to?'

'That'll do from you. I'll thank you not to speak to me, after the way you behaved.'

'How did I behave, may I make so bold as to inquire?' he said, flinging himself on the bed with his hands under his head and his shoes on the eiderdown.

The insolence of the act, the insolence of his speech, enraged Annie.

'Leaving *me*, your *wife*, in the street and walking off with some filthy woman, and I can find my way home as best I can. And in you come, hours later, cool as you please, without even a word of apology. If that's what you think proper behavior for a honeymoon, I don't.' She began slamming round the room, picking things

148

up meaninglessly and throwing them down elsewhere.

'That's nothing to get worked up about,' he said lazily. 'I can explain who — '

'I don't want to hear! I don't want to hear your explanations!' she cried, clapping her hands over her ears. 'All filthy lies every word of it! Think I don't know a bad lot when I see one?' But on the contrary, it was the grandeur of the wretched woman, the splendid fur coat, the velvet hat, that ground her heart with jealousy.

'You don't need to be jealous of Grace — ' laughed the man on the bed.

'Jealous!' the woman's laughter flared like twigs under a pot. 'I wouldn't be jealous of that! I don't trouble my head about her. It's you I'm disgusted with. I feel I don't ever want to see you again!'

'What? Just because I stop to speak to a girl half your age?' said Bates, in mock surprise. 'What you up to now?'

Finding a shoe and a pair of stockings in one hand and a brush in the other, decided her. 'Packing,' she said, and thrust them into a bag with trembling hands. She could have cried. At her age, to be so humiliated.

'I never knew a woman with such a jealous nature as yours, Annie. Fancy creating like this just because a feller stops to say a word to his sister he hasn't seen for two years.'

'Sister! You dirty blackguard!' she croaked, on her knees by the trunk, into which her heavy tears were falling, falling.

He sat bolt upright on the bed, suddenly venomous.

'You calling me a liar, Annie Marsh? The last person who done that swallered the word and some of his teeth too. See? I don't take that from anyone, wife or who the hell. See? Now, you just stop making a fool of yourself,' he said, pulling her up by her shoulders to face him, and seeing with satisfaction the tear stains on her cheek. 'Get it into your head that that girl was my sister. The reason I didn't want to introduce you then and there was, first, they don't know I'm married, and second, we quarreled two years ago and haven't seen or heard of one another since; I wasn't any too sure she'd speak to me. I wasn't going to take you across to be cut by her. I got some respect for my wife. However, it turned out she was quite chatty, and we'll be seeing her tomorrow. I told her we was married, and she asked you along to tea. She wants to meet you. We've made it up; so how about you and me making it up, eh?'

'I don't know about that,' Annie said stiffly. It was always difficult for her to come out of a temper.

Bates, who had never the patience himself to cajole people into good humor again, made a big gesture of inviting her to the cinema where she could be soothed out of her bitterness.

At ten past three, well into the big picture, he murmured an excuse and pushed past her. She took her eye off Hedy Lamarr, with tears like electric light bulbs hanging from her lashes, just long enough to glimpse him pushing through the door marked Gentlemen in luminous green glass and then turned her attention to Miss Lamarr's brave broken words and wounded heart. She could have cried for her . . .

At a quarter past three, Bates was back

in the boardinghouse, taking the stairs two at a time. It did not take him long to pack his few garments; and not very much longer to prod and poke among her things for the pieces of jewelry so carefully concealed. As they flashed in the palm of his hand so they flashed in his heart. His smile was a thin dark line across his face. He spread a half sheet of paper on the corner of the wash stand, licked his pencil stub, thought, and wrote:

Dear Annie,

I have been called away sudden. I would have told you about it except you seemed a bit ratty with me and I come to the conclusion it was kinder to slip away quiet and not spoil our happiness together by talking of sad things. I have much regret in informing you my poor father is dying and has expressed a wish to see me. I do not know how long I will be away as it depends how long it takes to settle his affairs, but I will not be returning to Selsey so do not wait for me.

Do not worry, dear Annie, about

your Jewelry which I know what store you set by it. I have only borrowed it, not having the cash for the journey north, my money being overdue from the Bank of Australia as you know. Will write and let you know what day I am returning, do not worry.

Hoping that Fate will not part us long.

Your own Boy,
Johnny

He grinned at himself in the glass, jaunty with self-satisfaction, and passed a brush briskly across his hair. Not a bad-looking guy, he decided, glancing at his reflection sideways. He passed a hand amorously over his breast pocket feeling the little bosses raised by the rings, the brooches, the eardrops, and their rough caress gave him a sensation akin to the ecstasy of self-love. He could not help chuckling at the thoughts which came flying into his head. They had nothing to do with Annie: she had ceased to exist for him . . .

11

I Only Want to Be Happy

Clouds obscured the pale tinfoil glitter of the sun on the gray water. The sea spread out its embroideries on the shingle for an instant and then whisked them away. On the bare edge of the shore crouched a huddle of bungalows bright with paint. They looked as fragile as if the wind could blow them apart, blow off the roofs and expose within rigid china inhabitants reclining obliquely on chairs, regarding with indifference the splendid fare spread before them, the *papier maché* lobster, the strawberry tarts, the pink and white cardboard ham . . .

But the bungalows did not seem absurd or pathetic to Grace; they seemed immensely desirable. They represented to her the peak of marital intimacy, the snugness of marital bliss. She envied Doris and Frank.

She hurried along the rough wind-blown road to 'Sea Haven,' holding on her hat. She did wonder excitedly what Doris would find to say to her news. She had been certain all along (underneath her despair, that is) that Freddy would come back to her one day. For hadn't she known from the first that they were fated — ever since he had rescued her from the sea — and their destiny would bring them together again . . . until death did them part!

As soon as Grace set foot in the house Doris spotted that something was up. She wasn't kept long in suspense. Grace leaned back against the door and said dramatically, 'Doris, who do you think I saw? You'll never guess!'

'That man,' said Doris imperturbably, flicking the ash off her eternal cigarette with a very telling gesture.

'It *was* Freddy! However did you guess?'

'I don't need to be a magician when you come in all flushed up like a kid at a party. What did he want?'

'He was looking for me. Truly. He said so. He just came up and said, 'Hello,

Grace,' not a bit surprised or anything. My goodness, I went like a jelly all over!'

'You're a jelly all right,' said Doris disgustedly in her haughty Oxford accent. 'I suppose you fell into his arms. You ought to have slapped his face, the blackguard!'

'But I was angry at first; before he explained. And I know he was speaking the truth. He'd been looking for me everywhere.'

'Why didn't he look for you where he might be expected to find you — at your home?' said Doris, raising her reddish brows.

'He did, as a matter of fact. And he wrote, like he promised.'

Grace turned away to take off her hat and fluff out her hair, and said in a subdued voice, 'It was Daddy who sent him away and said I wasn't there. And I suppose Daddy tore up the letters so I shouldn't see them. I think it was beastly of him . . . ruining my life. I feel I never want to speak to him again.'

'Well, we can easily find out the truth of that little story. All we need do is ring up your father and ask him.'

'I've told you, I don't want to speak to him again,' said Grace sulkily.

'I don't mind speakin' for you. I'd like a word with your dad about this, anyway.'

'Doris, you're not to! It's not fair! It's none of his business what I do now — I'm over thirty and married, I can do as I like.'

Doris flung down the cutlery in dismay. 'You're goin' back to him, then. You're goin' back to this horrible man who treated you so badly. How can you be such a fool!' she cried angrily, her small blue eyes sparkling.

'Of course I'm going back to him. Why are you all so against us?'

'No one's against *you*, darlin'. It's this ghastly Freddy of yours we don't trust.'

'I tell you he's explained everything.'

'All right! Let's give your dad a chance to explain his side of it!'

'Do you think I could believe a word he says after this?'

'You're hopeless!' cried Doris.

'And I was so happy when I came in,' blubbed Grace. 'Why are you so unkind?'

'My sweet child, it's for your own good! If you weren't as weak as water you'd see it for yourself as a hopeless proposition. If he's tellin' the truth and he really has been lookin' for you, it's because he wants somethin' more out of you and he knows you're easy money. And when he's got it, he'll slide out again, the way he did before.' She banged the dishes on the table, and drew up two chairs.

Grace sat up and blew her nose haughtily. 'I don't want any lunch, thank you . . . You don't know Freddy; if you did you wouldn't talk like that about him. But you can tell him just what you think this afternoon. I asked him here to tea.'

'I'm damned' exclaimed Doris, tipping the spoonful of cottage pie onto the table, in her confusion, instead of onto the plate.

'Now look what you've done!'

'Never mind! Do come and sit down!'

'I said I don't want any lunch, thank you. And it may interest you to know that I have already mentioned to Freddy that Granny's money has been tied up so I can't touch it.'

'And, my God, how right the old lady

was, as it turns out!'

'You see!' Grace said wildly. 'It doesn't matter what I say, you twist it to look bad against Freddy somehow. I thought you'd be on my side, Doris,' she added reproachfully.

'I am on your side, ol' girl, make no mistake about it.'

'I only want to be happy,' wailed Grace, weeping fast into her cottage pie as she ate.

'Look, you're givin' me indigestion! And how can I be on my dignity when I'm belchin' into your hubby's face?'

Grace giggled through her tears. Doris was being funny again. Everything would be all right.

Conversing lightly on other subjects over luncheon, Doris had time to get hold of herself and handle the business a little more tactfully.

'You knock up one of your nice sponges for tea, Grace,' she suggested. Presently she came back into the kitchen buttoning a clean blouse. 'Marvelous light hand you've got,' she blarneyed, watching her mix.

'It's easy,' said Grace, whisking the paste about with a carefree air. 'It's just knack, you know.'

'Look, Grace, you're not goin' to make up your mind about this thing in a hurry, are you? I mean, it doesn't ever do to let a man think he's only got to lift his little finger for you to come runnin'. Keep him hangin' about a bit. Do him good. They don't ever respect you if you're too easy, you can take it from me, dear. I've had a lot of experience and I'm a good deal older than you are; I know a thing or two,' she promised.

Grace straightened up from the oven with a flushed face. 'But, Doris, I already have made up my mind. I told Freddy. He's going to take me away tonight!'

* * *

Freddy arrived soon after four, all smiles and looking quite the gentleman. Grace could not but feel proud of him. She no longer doubted he would win Doris over. Doris was cool and unforthcoming. She had gone into one of her remote silences.

160

She gave him a nod, but did not unfold her arms.

He sat down, impervious to the atmosphere, and crossed one foot on his knee to show his dainty socks. He drummed stubby fingers nonchalantly on the arm of his chair, unperturbed by the silence into which his remarks fell. Grace hovered nervously.

An idea occurred to him. He dug thumb and forefinger into his breast pocket like a Hatton Garden merchant and took out something that quickly flashed in his grasp.

'Here!' he said, passing it to Grace. 'How do you like that?'

'Pretty, isn't it?' Grace admired Annie Grun's brooch with the special devout look women use for jewelry. She held it so that the light played on it; held it at arm's length, and against her sleeve; held it out to Doris.

'I thought you'd like it,' he said smugly. 'Soon as I saw it I said to myself, that's just Grace's style.' He watched Doris out of the corner of his eye. 'Go on,' he said, 'aren't you going to put it on?'

Grace flushed. 'You want me to wear it?' she ventured.

'Just as you like,' he shrugged. 'It's yours.'

'*Mine?*'

'Why not? Any law against a husband giving his wife a present?' He laughed loudly and winked at Doris.

'Oh, Freddy . . . Freddy! I can't believe it! How marvelous you are to me! It's lovely! Isn't it lovely, Doris . . . ? I shall always wear it, as long as I live,' she vowed in broken, sentimental tones; 'the first thing you ever gave me.' She put her arms round his neck and held up to him her naked shapeless mouth, whose feel he had forgotten. He dared not flinch before Doris. He closed his eyes quickly and bent to her face.

'Oh, Freddy!' she sighed, and reluctantly unloosed her hold. 'It's a sort of reunion present, isn't it?'

'If you like. Or a bonus on the money you lent me.'

'Oh, darling! Fancy bothering about that!' she said enraptured. That would show Doris! 'Has your invention been successful then?'

'Not too bad!' he said modestly. 'Tell you about that when we're alone.'

'I'll go and make tea,' said Doris, lifting herself out of her chair, and padding lightly from the room. You could really hear just as well in the kitchen what was being said in the room next door. But all Doris could hear was silence. Either they were embracing or Grace was silently mouthing a message — about Doris, very likely, and it would not be too hard to guess what.

The lovebirds were holding hands dumbly when she came back. Doris poured out languidly. She took no tea herself, but leaned back watching them and puffed out a cloud of smoke.

'How strange,' she smiled, 'that you should run into Grace like that — after all this time, too!'

Bates smirked. He was not so easily trapped. His line, whenever he was in doubt what to answer, was, 'Grace and me understand one another,' with a sidelong glance at his moonfaced girl fingering her brooch.

Doris, her eyes half-closed against the smoke of her cigarette, looked like a huge cat, her wild reddish hair sleeked back from her big white face. She could see, though she did not respond to, the creature's attraction. His stiff gestures and laconic phrases, in contrast with his odd look of frailty, the fan of lashes shading his hollow eyes, made of him a pathetically appealing figure that nine women out of ten would want to mother. But if he had the defiant look of a lost child, it was at the same time the sort of child who tears live insects apart leg by thready leg.

'So you want to take Grace away from us?'

'Any objection?'

'It's nothin' to do with me, I know. But Grace's parents are goin' to be a bit upset about it, I think. If I may give an opinion, I think Grace would be very unwise to go into this without informin' them beforehand.'

'Well, that's up to Grace, isn't it? If she feels she don't want any more interference between us, I can't say I blame her.'

'Why must it all be decided in such a hurry?'

'I don't see what there is to decide, if

you'll pardon me saying so. My wife and I get parted under circumstances over which we have no control, and after me wasting a lot of time and money I find her again: aren't we going to carry on where we left off? What else is there to decide, once she's made up her mind to come back to me?'

'Well, for one thing, you've got to decide where you're going once you walk out of here, haven't you? I think you'll find Grace won't be so keen this time to get landed in a dingy room in some back street of London.'

He darted a quick look at his wife, who flushed.

'No one's said anything about London. I've told Grace I'm agreeable to go anywhere she fancies.'

'Well, you can't get on a train to 'Anywhere', can you?' jeered the woman sarcastically. 'You must know where you want to go.'

'Say where you'd like to go, Gracie,' he urged.

But Grace had turned shy; she didn't know, or she wouldn't or couldn't say.

'Plenty of time to decide that later,' Bates said largely, shrugging.

Doris rested her eyes on Grace.

'You could have the 'Picaroo,' you know; it's to let.'

'The 'Picaroo' is? How wonderful, Doris! What a marvelous idea! How I should love that!'

'What's the 'Picaroo'?'

'It's the bungalow next door, darling. Wouldn't it be fun to be next to Doris and Frank, too?'

He sought for objections.

Doris said, 'Since you don't mind where you go, here's as good as anywhere else, isn't it? And Grace would find it ever so easy to run.'

'Oh Freddy, we must. Think of being able to pop out of the front door and have a swim before breakfast; wouldn't it be lovely? I just love living by the sea!' she gushed.

'We'll see.'

'No, but Freddy, why shouldn't we? You did say anywhere, and I was to choose. Well, I have chosen.'

'We'll have to see what it's like, et cetera.'

'Let's go now,' she said childishly.

The front door banged and droopy Frank peered round the door.

'Darlin', come in!' cried Doris. 'This is Grace's husband.'

'Well, well, well!' remarked Frank, shifting his umbrella to the other hand so that he could shake hands. And even then he was not sure whether the man was to be welcomed or not, so he repeated, 'Well, well, well!'

Grace, all impatience, hauled Bates by the arms, and explained to Frank that they were just off to look over the 'Picaroo.'

'You're too late!' warned Frank dolefully.

'Too late?' She could have wept.

'The estate agent's shut at five and it's after that now,' he said, drawing out his watch.

'Oh, you frightened me, Frank! I thought you meant it was already let. We needn't bother about the old house agent tonight. We can just walk over and look through the windows. Come on, Freddy . . . We won't be long,' she promised. 'Look, Frank, what Freddy's given me,' she said proudly.

'Very handsome!' he said, blinking at it, astonished that this common little man should have such good taste.

'Picaroo' through the windows had the derelict air of a dwelling that is only kept for letting; the furniture was of the flimsiest; sea-faded chintzes draped deal frames and meager Indian rugs made stepping stones across the concrete floors. In high summer it might look fresh and airy, now it looked depressingly shabby and chill. But Grace was enchanted with it; the kitchen with its tiny cooker, the pale blue plates ranged along the white dresser, the rows of bright canisters and glinting saucepans had for her all the allure of the toy shops of her childhood and held the promise of delightful 'games.' It would be just like being grown-up.

Bates neither liked nor disliked it. His only care was to weigh the disadvantages against the advantages. He liked its isolated position, he liked its being so near the sea, from a queer irrational notion that Grace having come to him out of the sea might be lost to him in the same way, might drown and be lost to him forever. What he disliked, however, was Doris' nosiness; neighbours were all very well so long as they didn't interfere.

'I had thought of taking you somewhere better than this,' he said fastidiously. 'Now that you got money too we could go somewhere really posh.'

'I haven't actually got my money yet, Freddy, so we don't know quite how much it will be. About £300 a year, they say. Granny's only been dead about two months and there's something called Probate, which I don't understand. Anyway, Mr. Hewbank, the solicitor, gave me some money out of his own pocket and I'll pay him back later.'

'How much did he give you?'

'A hundred. But I've only got twenty left; this coat cost fifty-five, and I've bought odds and ends, and I pay Doris two pounds a week for my keep.'

'He'll let you have more when you want it.'

'Will he?' she said doubtfully.

'We'll go and see him,' Bates said confidently.

'We're going to see the agent first thing tomorrow,' cried Grace when they came back. She and Doris at once became immersed in domestic conversation.

Frank broached a few careful remarks.

'Where are you staying?'

'Haven't fixed up anywhere, 's'marrerfact.'

'I'm sorry we haven't a bed to offer you here,' Frank said politely.

'Oh, that's all right, I can doss with Grace.'

'I'm afraid you wouldn't be very comfortable. It's a very narrow divan.'

'Oh, I can doss down anywhere; a cushion on the floor will do me okay, an old soldier's used to roughing it.'

12

No Bequests

The next day Grace paid over a month's rent in advance, in lieu of references, so that they could move in immediately. As soon as Doris had seen them making for Selsey she sat down to write to Mrs. Pickering to tell her what had happened.

My dear Agnes [she scribbled in her large untidy calligraphy,]

You will be as sorry to hear as I am to tell you that that rotter has turned up again. I do not know how he managed to find her. His story was that he had been on the lookout for her all the time and that he went to 'Blue Windows' for her but was *prevented from seeing her!* I am sure this is not true, but if it is, then I must say I am on your side. You know Grace, she has fallen into his arms. She would swallow any tale he told her and won't hear a word against him. She *is* potty about him, isn't she? I suppose it's all right, while it lasts, and always providing he treats her decently.

My dear, I tried, but I couldn't stop the little fool walking off with him. All I could do was suggest them renting the bungalow next door, so as I could keep an eye on Grace and see she isn't made too unhappy . . .

It was natural for Doris to write to Grace's mother since it was not Grace but Mrs. Pickering who was Doris' friend. She had taken in Grace more to oblige Agnes than anything else; sorry the girl had made such an unfortunate marriage and was still moping about it six months later. Agnes and she were old but not close friends, and although they lived within reasonable visiting distance they seldom saw one another. They corresponded infrequently too, just enough to keep in touch. To be honest, Doris faintly despised the older woman for her hen-like indecision; but she was a little too afraid of Mr. Pickering to write direct to him. Agnes would certainly show him the letter.

Grace also wrote home, without waiting for Freddy's advice this time.

Dearest Mumples [she wrote],

Freddy has come back to me. He has explained everything and I am very happy. I hope you will come and see us (we have taken this dear little bungalow next door to Doris'), but I think it would be better if Daddy didn't come just yet as Freddy feels very hurt at the unfair way he has been treated.

Freddy has given me a beautiful diamond brooch, real diamonds. He has had a great success with his invention and does not need my money, which Daddy seemed to think he was after. I am very happy, so I hope no one will try to come between us again.

With much love,
from your devoted daughter,
Grace

The letter Bates wrote at this time was to the lawyers who handled Grace's grandmother's affairs, commanding them to send him 'a copy of the will for his perusal.' Until he saw the terms it was couched in he could not hope to know whether it could be broken. There must be some way of getting at that wealth of gold, and if there were it would be his pleasure to discover it.

Two days after Grace's letter home, she was absolutely astonished to see her father's little Austin chug up outside the gate of 'Picaroo' — as if this visitation was the most unlikely thing in the world! She ran into the bedroom, where Bates was still lying in bed:

'Freddy, Freddy! What do you think? Daddy's here!'

'Christ!' he exclaimed, and sprang to his feet. 'What's he want? Come to take you away! Put the bolt on the door, Grace, quick!'

'I haven't unlocked it yet. But, why — '

'Lock the back door, then. Don't let him in till I say! Go *on*, Grace, don't stand there *gaping!*'

She scrambled away and came back to find him standing behind the sitting-room curtains squinting out.

'Your mother's here too,' he whispered.

'But what are we going to do, Freddy? Aren't I to let them in?'

'Let 'em think we're out!'

'Oh, Freddy, how unkind! We can't.'

He turned on her a furious face. 'Well, what d'you think they've come for: to tell you how glad they are you're going to be happy in spite of all they done to prevent it? They've come to try and get you away! Don't you see? They're just out to come between us again; they'll never let us alone, you'll see, unless we *show* 'em.'

'Daddy will be so angry,' murmured Grace, her eyes dilating at the furious sound of the knocker, the persistent shrilling of the bell. ('Grace! Open this door!')

'If I let him in there'd only be a roughhouse. You know how I feel about the rotten way your father's behaved toward me. And you wouldn't want to see him beaten up, any more than you would me, I suppose.'

The back door was attacked. She stood in the hail and saw her father's and mother's faces pressing against the kitchen window, like unhappy aquaria, as they tried to see within. But the goggling eyes and green triangles of flesh did not make her want to laugh; she was too rattled for that.

She sucked in her breath, went across and opened one window a few inches.

'Daddy, it's no use, I can't let you in. It would only mean you having a terrible row with Freddy.'

'Grace, don't be an idiot! Open this door at once!'

'I did tell you not to come, in my letter.'

'Grace, will you please open this door!'

'What do you want?' she said uneasily.

'To speak to you of course. Grace, this has been a great shock to your mother, and to me. You shouldn't have done it. At least let us talk it over. If you're afraid to let us in, come outside and let us talk to you there.'

Grace opened her mouth to reply but suddenly disappeared from the window. The window slammed shut.

Bates said irately, his face patched with

red, 'I told you to let 'em think we was out, *didn't I?*'

The shadows at the window vanished. Presently the Pickerings went down the path, hesitated, and then crossed over to 'Sea Haven' and were lost to sight. The Austin did not move from outside the gate till late afternoon, and the Pickerings did not appear again until they left. Neither Grace nor Bates dared venture out till they had gone, nor even unlock the doors. It was like a siege. And as in a siege, nervous excitement was interspersed with long periods of boredom and restlessness. By afternoon, Bates was as touchy as a cat that has been stroked too much. And Grace, between wanting to be consoled and reassured, wanted to know what they had come for, wanted the conversation repeated to her again and again, like a gramophone, with a gramophone's mechanical precision too. This childish craving for the story to be repeated and repeated had been all right with Mumples but was very far from all right with the irascible Bates.

Even Doris refused to discuss the

Pickerings' visit afterward.

It soon became forgotten. Grace was far too busy to dwell in the past. She was discovering at last what it was like to be a real married woman, a wife. Like a child pretending to an adult's burdens, she seriously assumed the delicious responsibilities of running a house and pleasing her husband. As yet she could not understand how some women were thankful to see their husbands go off to work; she was sure she should be dreadfully lonely if Freddy were not there, and *she* was thankful he did not go out to work. Besides the past had left her with a legacy of unease, to wonder if she would ever see him again, whenever he was out of her sight for a few minutes. So much so, that she rarely did let him go anywhere without her. It was not as if he were a drinking man who wanted to go into a pub every evening; there was really nothing now for him to be away for. They knew no one in Selsey apart from Doris and Frank. If he desired male companionship he could talk to Frank, while she talked to Doris. It was ideal. They were together all the time; and in such a tiny little house it really was all the time, for it was not possible for one to make the smallest, discreet movements without being heard by the other.

He could not shake her off. He had only to fling aside his newspaper and say he thought he would take a walk, for her to spring gaily up from whatever she was doing to accompany him. He had never married anyone who made such insatiable demands upon his attention. She had to know what he was thinking all the time. Yet was the way she never let his mind alone any worse than the way she never let his sacred person alone? She was forever touching him; and that was something he could not endure. If he snarled out at her, as his exacerbated nerves often led him to do, she burst into tears and then there was a scene, and the scene was only to be ended with more caresses and kisses. There was no way out. His sole prayer was that it would not be for long.

The grandmother's will he had taken to a local solicitor to see if there was any way of getting at the capital. The solicitor had advised Counsel's Opinion, and on the strict understanding that Grace would pay for it (after all, it was for her that he was trying to get the money, he explained), Bates agreed.

That took three weeks; so that altogether he had endured Grace for a month. And then when Counsel's Opinion came it was implacably unfavorable: the capital could not be broached until the terms of the trust ended with Grace Noble's death.

From that moment Grace's life was not worth the purchase.

It was obvious that Grace would live forever. Despite her ditheriness, her parasitical dependency would long outlast Bates's taut nerve-strung egotism. Even his limited powers of fancy could work up an image of Grace as a fat and foolish old lady, all trembling chins and smiles from watery eyes — disgusting!

Still, he had not gone to the length of killing her — even in his mind, until Grace timidly, carelessly, dropped her thunderbolt, as if it were an eggshell.

In an unusually sour mood even for him, he had been nagging on about the money indirectly; about Mr. Hewbank, Grace's solicitor, directly; fretting that he was unreliable; suggesting he had, or was about to, abscond with the money . . .

'Oh, he wouldn't!' Grace had protested. 'He's not like that a bit, truly, darling. He's a sweet old man.'

What did she know about it, pray? Had she seen him?

Artlessly, incredibly artlessly even for her, Grace had said, 'I naturally had to see him when I went up to make my will.'

There was a pause, and then he said, his eyes resting on her thoughtfully, 'First I heard of you making a will. When was this?'

She said hurriedly, 'Oh, darling, it was before you came back,' and flushed a deep unbecoming burgundy as the implications latent in her words became apparent to her.

As they became apparent to Bates he turned the tallowy white of a candle. He stared at her with such a look that she put her hands up to her cheeks in fright.

'I didn't know you were ever coming back to me then,' she explained beseechingly. 'They *made* me do it, Freddy, they said I'd *got* to make a will. Who else was I to leave my money to but Daddy and Mumples? I can easily alter it.' Freddy had blindly scrunched up an antimacassar from the chair back he was leaning over and was wringing it between his hands in a way that made her tremble. The stream of abuse muttered between his teeth hardly penetrated her mind; all her alarmed attention was on the cruel grip of those hands. In more wholesome English, he was calling her a swindling liar to have deliberately tried to cheat him.

'Freddy, I didn't! I forgot all about it. I swear!' she agonized.

He laughed; and she covered her ears from the sound.

He flicked a corner of the antimacassar at her sharply across one cheek and then the other.

'Keep your money,' he advised her with his straight-lipped ugly grin. 'I'm through.' And he turned and left the room.

She ran after him sobbing, '*Freddy!*'

He was in the bedroom, his suitcase open on the bed.

'No, Freddy! *Please! Don't go! I can alter it! Freddy, listen to me! I can alter it! Freddy, darling! Please!*'

After a most exhausting scene he allowed himself to be won round. He agreed at last that she should alter her will in his favor. She wrote to Hewbank asking for an appointment. Bates accompanied her to the office and was introduced to Mr. Hewbank the senior partner, a rosy old man with eyes of steel. It was Bates's idea to make it appear that they had come up to get a further advance on the money Grace was to receive. Bates bickered rather futilely in an attempt to ante him up to a further two hundred and fifty, whereas Hewbank was not prepared to advance more than a hundred and fifty — and that would mean that the first year's income would go straight into his pocket and they wouldn't see another penny of it. Bates sucked in his lips and looked sullen, as if he was being done down and knew it but was too polite to say so. He jerked his chin at Grace and she plunged forward into her prepared speech.

'Oh, Mr. Hewbank, while we're here — I want to make my will. A new will, I mean. I'm not satisfied the old one is fair, now my husband and I are together again.'

'You want to leave something to him, is that it? We can add a codicil, you know; it will not be necessary to create an entirely new will.'

Grace looked baffled and Bates hastily cut in, 'But what my wife and me want is to leave everything to one another.'

'Mutually favorable wills, is that it?' He looked at Bates acutely. 'That is what you want?'

'That is what my wife wants, and I've agreed with her.'

'You do quite understand, Mrs. Noble, that if you should die before your husband your parents would not benefit at all?'

Grace looked uneasy.

Again Bates cut in, 'What Grace feels is that they done their level best to come between us and break up our marriage;

and it's sort of turned her against them.'

'Indeed! Then your wish is, Mrs. Noble, to leave your entire estate to your husband — '

'And I leave my entire estate to her,' put in Bates.

Mr. Hewbank ignored him.

'And no bequests?'

'No bequests,' repeated Grace, nodding her head.

With the utmost indifference Mr. Hewbank scribbled some remarks on a little pad in front of him and told Grace he would send her the drafts to approve as soon as they were prepared. His indifference seemed hardly courteous; they were dismissed from the room like ill-mannered schoolchildren.

13

It Doesn't Look Well to Be So Damned Callous

About this time Doris began to change her mind about Frederick; though she still did not personally like him it did seem that he was devoted to Grace, he fussed over her in a way that would have maddened Doris but which obviously made Grace *glisten* with pleasure. And it did not seem put on for their benefit; if she was out of his sight for five minutes he became restless and absurdly anxious: one would imagine to hear him talk that Grace was a child of five alone in the streets for the first time. It was really rather touching.

The four of them were on reservedly friendly terms. Two or three times a week they spent evenings in one another's homes, usually playing whist or rummy. As far as Bates was concerned, it passed the time pleasantly — he had a flair for cards — and at least freed him for an hour or two from the dreadful necessity of listening to Grace's maddening prattle. Conversation, when conversation there was, was scrupulously divided between Doris and Grace on the one hand and Bates and Frank on the other; it never became general.

While the women chattered of clothes and food in happy intimacy, the two men roved awkwardly from one subject to another searching for common ground. Bates's range was limited, and besides one never knew what snag one might suddenly run up against, how unwittingly one might give oneself away. However, he had necessarily bummed around a good deal in his 'business' life, and the English country — or seaside — towns he had stayed in at different times were always a suitable topic. Frank, on the other hand, had practically never been anywhere other than his native Harrogate before he was sent down south (he had never acclimatized himself to Selsey and the unfriendly southerners), and Frank was only too happy to talk of the charms of Harrogate for hours — it was a way of picking up the past again. Bates smiled, half-listening to him, half-listening to the women, and thinking his thoughts . . .

Weeks passed, and nothing came from Hewbank. Grace wrote to him, under Bates's instructions. Another week went by: no answer. Grace wrote again. At long last an answer came apologizing for the delay and explaining that he had been away from the office, ill, and now that he was back in harness he was very busy with arrears of work; her business would be attended to at the first opportunity.

They heard nothing more.

The thing was, Bates simply could not go on hanging about any longer. The life he was living, the haunting pile of money there just out of his reach, ravaged him. He *suffered*. And then there was the perpetual dread that something would happen to Grace before she had made the new will.

What one has done once one can do again, and now he busied his mind with restless schemes for 'getting rid' of her. He seemed more abstracted than ever.

'Now what are you thinking?' Grace would say, ruffling his soft dark locks. And he would look up at her with a dreamy absent smile, blinking a little, to reply candidly, 'You.'

He was like an author struggling with an obstinate plot. There were certain lines he was determined to keep to. It was to be an 'accident.' That was the only safe way; there was no question then about disposing of the body — that terrible problem. Also, he must not be present himself; for two reasons: one: that he desired the reassurance of an alibi, and two: that he did not like to see suffering. He was afraid of it in some way; could never bring himself to lay hands on another person. He would always kill like a woman; not for him the bludgeon, the axe, the strangling grasp of bare hands. In truth, his hatred of life was so intense and venomous that if he had expressed it in the violence he felt inwardly, his feelings would soon have passed beyond his control. He was aware of this in some profound subconsciousness and therefore repressed it in his consciousness till it was only a vivid horror of violence.

His mind always turned first to electricity, since it was one thing of which he had acquired rudimentary knowledge. Its fascination for him was that an electric shock was so natural an 'accident.' The Titmuss gambit could not be used because there was no telephone at 'Picaroo.' Just as well perhaps; even Bates knew that it was the murderer's rigid adherence to formula which so often roused people's suspicions.

Gradually an idea evolved in his rattrap brain. It was midsummer now and warm enough for Grace to indulge in a dip before breakfast. She liked to spend most of the day sunning on the beach and plunging in and out of the water. Bates did not swim.

The floors at 'Picaroo' were concrete. A wonderful piece of luck! But the switches were plastic and that would not do. One day when Grace was next door, he cracked one switch with a hammer blow. He made rather a fuss about it being broken when she came back; said it was dangerous, said he would complain to the landlord. And he did in fact complain insolently to the agent, demanding that it be attended to at once. So it was hardly surprising it was not seen to. And Bates said he supposed he'd have to do it himself. Grumbling loudly he set out to get what he wanted. Actually, although he grudged the money, he knew he would have to put new switches in all the rooms; one brass one among all the plastics would stand out too remarkably; if they were all of brass no one would notice that they had been freshly fixed.

He went ahead with these preparations at once because he was still expecting daily to hear from Hewbank with a draft of the new will. It took him all one afternoon, whistling gaily in his shirt sleeves, to replace the switch covers. The bathroom one he kept to do while Grace was occupied in preparing the supper; that was a little more trouble. Before he began work on it he went down to the sea for a 'breath of fresh air,' and came back with some sea water in a half-pint milk bottle. When he had removed the plastic cover on the bathroom switch, he sprinkled sea water on the insulating board inside, and then screwed on the new brass cover. He was very blithe that evening over supper and made jokes.

Secretly, every other day or so, he repeated the process.

The thought of getting rid of Grace exhilarated him almost as much as the thought of the money he would get from her death. He had disliked her from the first, and had built up a tower of petty resentments against her.

But as time passed he became very agitated and edgy at not receiving that damned will from the solicitors. There was so little time left now, that even to go to a local solicitor would take too long — solicitors were so infernally slow, unless they knew it was a matter of life and death (and he could hardly admit it to be that!). The only thing left for him to do was to write it himself. If he hesitated it was not from qualms about his ability to create a watertight will — he knew the law! — it was the problem of finding two witnesses that held him back. They knew no one locally (unluckily he had made that sure himself) except for Doris and

Frank, and they were the last people he wanted to witness the will. Even with his insane assurance he could see it would not look well to them if Grace should die a few days after they had witnessed her new will; that would be too much.

Meanwhile crusts of blue-green corrosion were forming inside the switch. Bates was getting frantic.

And then his opportunity came. Just the fluke he had been praying for. The dustmen visited those outlying parts only at long intervals, and as a result Bates had not given them a thought until he saw them actually plodding up the path. He sprang up and shouted for Grace.

She ran in with a towel round her shoulders, her hair dripping.

'Freddy! Whatever is the matter? Calling like that, I thought something must have happened!'

'I'm going to make my will — *now*, and you had better make yours too, Grace.'

'Why, now, all of a sudden?' she protested.

'Because the dust cart is here and the

dustmen can be witnesses,' he said impatiently.

She laughed stupidly. 'How funny you are, Freddy! I can't do my will *now*, with my hair half washed.'

'Of course you can! Don't be silly, Grace! This is important. You must get some paper and sit down while I go and get the dustmen.'

He darted out to prevent them leaving. Grace could see him at the gate, arguing or explaining, and the men surly and immovable. She laughed a bit, inanely, at the strange fancies men got. Seeing them trooping up to the front door, she snatched up a blouse and thrust her arms in, doing it up as she went to let them in.

To cover their uncertainty the dustmen remained wiping their boots on the mat for a long time.

'Won't you come in?' said Grace sociably, as if they were visitors.

They exchanged glances.

'We can't stop,' warned one.

'You won't be long, will you, Mister?' nagged the other.

Bates had to verify the date, find a pen

that would write, hunt round for ink and paper, get out the shilling Encyclopedia and turn up the section on will-making and all the while the dustmen were fidgeting in the background and giving restless little coughs; so that by the time Bates had got all together he was in a lather, like an overridden horse. He was terrified they would leave before it was done. His hand was shaking so, that he spoiled two sheets of paper.

He wrote his own first, following the terminology of the Encyclopedia. It would look better.

'This is the last Will and Testament of me, Frederick Henry Noble of 'Picaroo,' Beach Edge, Selsey, in the county of Sussex, in which I hereby revoke all past wills made hitherto by me and give to my wife all my property whatsoever and appoint her my sole executor.'

He signed his name, added the date, and beneath that wrote:

'Signed in his presence and in the presence of each other,' and directed the dustmen how and where to attest it.

When they had signed it, he took a

fresh sheet of paper and wrote out Grace's will in identical terms; which she signed, the drips off the ends of her hair marking the paper with little water blisters.

He borrowed half a crown from her to tip the dustmen with. He could not have felt more benevolent if he had given them a five pound note — which of course was very unlikely. He was jovial with relief and pinched Grace's cheek to express his good humor.

It was done just in time too. A few days later when he touched the switch he felt a shock run up his arm. By now the sea water had sogged through the insulating board. The time left could only be brief. So he made his last arrangements. If he was silent and peevish when she broke in on his thoughts that Saturday it was because he had a great deal to go over in his mind, like an acrobat testing his ropes. Thus Grace's last day differed in no respect from the rest, and she was not rendered suspicious by any unexpected kindness from him.

★ ★ ★

The sun shone into his face next morning as he turned over in bed, waking him with a terrible start of fear that it was too late. Grace was up! She had drawn back the curtains and let in the bright day. He sprang out of bed and ran to look for her.

'Aren't you going to have your swim as usual?' he cried anxiously.

'Why, Freddy, of course not!'

He stared. 'Of course not! *Why* not?'

'Darling, it's Sunday.'

'Sunday! What's Sunday got to do with it?'

'I never bathe on Sunday. It wouldn't be right.'

'Why ever not, pray?' he demanded furiously.

'Because of religion,' she suggested in a hushed voice.

He recollected a saw that seemed to him doubly applicable.

'Better the day, better the deed,' he said cheerfully. 'You run on and have your nice swim. Go on! Don't be silly!'

But it was hard work persuading her.

She could be devilish obstinate when she chose. She had the notion it would offend the neighbours, and she had been brought up in the strict suburban consideration of neighbourly feelings.

'They don't any of them go to church round here, so why should they care if you have a swim as usual? It's all rot, my dear girl,' he said testily. 'Look here, at the time! Soon you'll be saying it's too late to go. Most of 'em'll be asleep now, I shouldn't wonder. You cut along, and I'll have breakfast ready when you get back.'

When he was in a sweet mood like that, she hardly liked to refuse for fear of upsetting him. Not that she wanted him to cook the breakfast and burn the bacon and mess up the stove, but she wouldn't have told him so for the world, he was so sensitive; not that she wanted to go bathing either, but if he had set his heart on it it was better to obey. She had already learned that whatever the cost to a woman, it was never worth upsetting the man. It was always easier to give in. Wiser to give in. She crammed her bush of hair inside a cap and ran barefooted down the path.

He hustled on his clothes. Turned off the main. Pressed down the bathroom switch, and turned the main on again. Now when Grace ran into the bathroom to cast off her wet suit and dry herself, she would see the light on. She would stare, puzzled perhaps, but she would certainly switch it off. And that would be that.

It was eight o'clock when he followed her down the path and paused outside 'Sea Haven.' Grace was already a long way out; there was no more of her to be seen than the crimson blob of her cap like a pinprick of blood on the creased blue silk of the water. She was certainly too far off to hear him if he called, but his voice would penetrate the thin walls of 'Sea Haven' and it was for the benefit of Doris and Frank that he slowly bawled seaward that he was going to fetch the morning papers and advised her considerately not to stay in too long.

At the bus junction about two miles down the road there was a small cafe which took in the Sunday papers for regular customers. He collected as usual the *News of the World* for himself and the *Sunday Graphic* for Grace. Too artful to be caught over a small thing like that. He ordered egg and beans on toast while he was waiting, and a cup of brownish liquid that was called tea or coffee according to what one ordered. Perhaps the walk had given him an appetite, at any rate, he enjoyed his first meal alone after so long, in spite of the business still to be done.

He got back at seven minutes past nine and stood inside the 'Picaroo' for a minute listening appreciatively to the silence. It was grand not to have someone rushing out at him like a great lolloping affectionate dog.

The light was still on in the bathroom and when he opened the door he saw Grace. He took the key from the inside, locked the door, and put the key in his pocket.

Frank and Doris were in their night clothes when he burst in on them and the sight of them gave him a sudden insane desire to laugh. He could feel his cheeks twitching dangerously and he put up his hands to cover his treacherous face. He took two stumbling steps forward.

He heard Doris cry out, 'What's the matter? For God's sake, what — '

'She's dead!' he said baldly. 'My wife's dead!' He took away his hands to stare at them. As they said nothing and the silence intimidated Bates, he elaborated nervously, 'I can't believe it. She was right as rain when I left her; she going off for a swim and me to get the papers, barely an hour ago. I dare say you saw her.'

'I saw her come back,' Doris said in a curious stony voice, 'while I was starting the coffee, not half an hour ago. She can't be dead!'

'She is though,' said Bates. 'It's been a terrible shock to me of course to be the one to discover the tragedy. But it doesn't do any good talking about that; what I want is for Frank to be a pal and come back with me and help me bust down the door. Grace having locked herself in.'

Doris sat up and whirled her silk wrapper round her shoulders in a beautiful gesture like the beginning of a dance. But above it her big white face was set in strong lines of terror, like a mask.

'I'm going to her,' she said. 'I don't believe it.'

'You don't want to lose your head. There's nothing you can do.'

'Wait, Doll,' advised her husband in a low tone, pulling on trousers, cramming his feet into shoes.

'How can he know she's dead, if she's locked in?' she muttered back.

'The light's on,' Bates explained hurriedly, 'and you can see as plain as plain through the window. It's that faulty switch done it, I know, which I told the agent he ought to get it seen to weeks ago. They never listen. I shall tell him he's responsible.'

'If you saw her through the window, why didn't you get to her that way?' said Doris slowly.

'I suppose I could have,' he said with a nervous smile, his eyes watchful. 'I never thought. Not that it would have made any difference; she must have been dead a long time.'

Doris went for a doctor, while they went to 'Picaroo.'

The door was only a plywood frame. A

child could have smashed it in easily. While Frank was turning off the main, Bates tucked the key back on the inside of the lock, for him to find who cared to look for it.

'My God,' said old Frank huskily, bowing his head. 'My God, how ghastly!'

'It's a quick death though, and you don't suffer, they say.'

Frank looked at him in horror and stammered out, 'Look here, Noble, there's no law that a chap who's just lost his wife is bound to give way to his feelings, however tragic the circumstances, but it doesn't look well to be as damned callous as you are.'

'I'm stunned,' said Bates glibly, 'that's what it is.'

Frank could not be expected to understand just what terrors Bates was fighting down. Bates's wooden nonchalance might strike the outsider as shocking indifference, but it was in itself a defense measure. To have allowed himself to realize what he had done would have been his ruin. And what he did not feel and dared not imagine, he could not simulate. Even had he been capable of simulating emotions he had not experienced, he would not have dared to feign grief now. For feigned grief might lead to real tears and real terror, and something in the back of his mind, great Biblical phrases they had threatened him with as a child might jump out and overthrow him with their thunderous Thou Shalt Nots.

So whatever funny ideas Frank and Doris got in their heads from talking over his odd behavior and the queer things he had said, there really was nothing to do about it, no proof that it was not a sheer accident. Undeniably Noble had not been near the house at the time. It was just an unfortunate concatenation of circumstances, the Coroner said, that the switch should be live and the deceased in her bare wet feet on the concrete floor have made herself a conductor. There was a reprimand for the agent, who should have had the faulty switch attended to after the husband's complaint; and sympathy was extended to the husband on his tragic loss.

Although Bates was delighted with

himself, he wisely slid out of Selsey before Pickering could lay hands on him.

A fortnight later he was alarmed to hear from the solicitor he had employed to prove the will that a caveat had been entered against it at Somerset House. That was that old devil Hewbank, God rot him! What was he up to? Could he have found anything, or was he just stalling for time?

Hewbank had been making investigations on behalf of Mr. Pickering and was hardly surprised to discover that the marriage was bigamous. Coincidentally with Grace's demise, he communicated the fact to the police. That alone would not have prevented Bates from benefiting under the will, but for a piece of criminal carelessness on his part in drafting the wills in his flustered haste that hot day. Unfortunately for him he had written: '*I give to my husband all my property whatsoever.*' He was not the poor woman's husband. If he had made her specify him by name . . . As it was, if he stretched out a hand for the money he might expect to feel a handcuff snap round his wrist, and to be arrested for bigamy. So it had all been for nothing.

The revenge was all Grace's.

14

Ruth and Me Are Going to Be Friends

They never traced what became of him after that. He disappeared for a while, to reappear like a toad when the climate was more favorable.

What finally brought him out of his cache was a piece in the paper, a front-page column in his favorite *News of the World*, as it happens. Synonyms for 'mental hospitals' and 'money' always leaped to his eye before all else nowadays, in the way that hitherto insignificant words do sometimes suddenly acquire a great meaning. What caught his eye this fine morning was the heading:

ASYLUM PATIENT 20 YEARS INHERITS
FORTUNE

Dark-haired Ruth Dunville, a slim petite woman of 42, an inmate of Lywood

Asylum, Hampshire, since 1927, as the last remaining member of the Dunville family, has become at the death of her sister, Barbara Dunville, last September, sole heiress to the Dunville estate of £60,000.

The firm of Dunville & Co. was wound up in 1932 on the death of Mayor Dunville. Makers of City pots for over two hundred years, they were the last firm to carry on this dying industry. In 1927 Charles Dunville, the then head of the firm, met his death in tragic circumstances on the tennis court of their country house. Miss Ruth Dunville, who witnessed the accident, held herself to blame for the fatality although exonerated by the Coroner. The shock of her favorite brother's sudden demise seriously affected her mental balance and she soon after became an inmate of Lywood Asylum where she has remained ever since. Quiet, attractive, and fond of gardening, Miss Dunville shows no inclination to return to the stresses of the world outside.

Charles Dunville when the fatality

occurred was engaged to Miss Lynette 'Bobs' Adam, who afterward married the Earl of Rustington.

He pored over this information till the cutting was limp and smudged. She sounded all right, though that was neither here nor there; it was worth being tied to a loony for life for sixty thousand pounds. Such a sum was beyond his imaginings. But even trying to comprehend it was enough to make him gloat. No family — that was the beautiful thing about it; no one to interfere. As he read it: this Dunville woman for one reason or another, probably jealousy, had done in her brother and then lost her head. His own superiority in this direction encouraged him to suppose that she'd be a cinch to handle: one word about Charles — !

Four days after he read the piece in the newspaper, he was on his way to Lywood in Hampshire. There was nearly half a mile of graveled drive to walk up before he came to the red brick hospital. The Matron in her green uniform with silver buttons looked like Mrs. Noah in pince-nez. Bates explained that he was a cousin of Miss Dunville's from Australia. He had not known any of the family were still alive until he read about Ruth in the paper. He'd just like to see that the poor girl was happy and had everything she wanted, and to tell her that she was not quite alone in the world.

The Matron looked dubious.

'Didn't her family come and see her when they were alive?' he asked.

'They did. But not often. Miss Dunville that died used to come two or three times a year.'

'Didn't Ruth used to recognize her then? Or was it that it upset her to see people?'

'Of course she would recognize her sister all right; but it does upset them very often to see their families and be reminded of the world outside and things they wish to forget.'

'Is she violent, then?'

'Oh, gracious, no! She's a melancholic. *Quite* quiet, too quiet, you know. They don't speak. But no, she's not violent.'

'I'm glad of that,' said Bates simply. He

stood up, 'Well, if I might just have a word with her.'

'If you'll excuse me a moment, then, I'll just see' — murmured the Matron as she bustled away on her twinkling black legs.

He hummed to himself thoughtfully and printed a pattern of dusty footmarks on the dark linoleum.

Matron returned after some minutes apologetically.

'I'm so sorry but Miss Dunville is not well enough to receive visitors today.'

'But I've come all this way!' he cried.

'Yes, such a pity! If you had let us know . . . but perhaps you weren't able to arrange for any other time . . . Poor Miss Dunville, she'll be sorry to have missed you,' the Matron politely lied, knowing that Miss Dunville's choice in the matter would always be not to see a stranger or indeed anyone who would talk to her about the past. 'Are you staying in England long?'

'Depends,' answered Bates absently. Suddenly he said briskly, 'Well, I'll come in tomorrow and see if she's well enough to see me. What would be the best time?'

The Matron was taken aback.

'Are you staying here then? I understood you were just passing through.'

'Having come so far to see my cousin, I reckon I might as well stay a few days if I have to in order to see for myself how she's getting on.' He looked at the Matron, and then suddenly volunteered, 'I feel I owe it to her family; they was good to me when I was young and Ruth and me were kids.'

'I hadn't understood that you knew her.'

'She mightn't remember me,' he said quickly.

'Oh, you must be prepared for that. After a time, you know, their memory becomes impaired.'

It was arranged that he should return about noon the next day. As it was fine and warm, the patients were in the garden. Matron conducted him there herself. He felt she would expect him to pick out Ruth Dunville as proof of his story and he gazed about him, searching for a slim petite dark-haired woman among the sauntering group of ill-looking women, some of whom gesticulated and talked aloud to themselves, answering unheard voices. One or two of them smiled at him and nodded affably, as though they recognized him.

Matron stood beside him on the steps, as quietly observant as a maître d'hôtel.

'There's Miss Dunville,' she said, pointing to a bench under a tree, on which were seated two women. One was a nurse in uniform, the other was a gaunt, middle-aged woman with ashen hair, drooping, eyes bent on the ground like a dull obedient child.

'Is that her?' Bates said in unconcealed dismay, so unlike was she to the picture he had conjured up from the newspaper report. He added truthfully, 'I should never have known her. Why's she got a nurse with her? I thought you said she wasn't dangerous.'

'Only to herself. I warned you she was not very fit just now, and when she has her bad times she is liable to do herself an injury; she is not safe to be trusted alone at such times. But Nurse Lockwood is well able to manage her; she's very fond of Nurse Lockwood.'

The nurse stood up at their approach,

but the person on the bench did not even lift her eyes, her spirit sealed with slumber.

Matron took up one of her limp hands and said in a special voice, 'Miss Dunville dear, here's a gentleman come all the way from Australia to see you. Are you going to give him a nice smile?'

Miss Dunville dear might have been in a trance for all the notice she took. When the Matron released her hand it fell back into her lap unresistingly.

'I don't think you'll get much response from her today, you know. But one never can tell, a fresh voice may rouse her. Try, by all means. But if you'll excuse me now . . . ' She trotted briskly through the aimlessly circulating women, who cried out and tried to claim her attention as she passed up the steps and through the swinging door.

For once in his life Bates felt helpless and ridiculous, standing in front of this inattentive woman, under the nurse's critical eye.

But Nurse Lockwood wasn't in the least critical. She was a friendly creature, quite 'a sport' off duty and even a little bit mad herself where the boys were concerned. So she gave Bates one of her friendly looks and said, 'Speak to her yourself, why don't you?'

Bates said, 'Hullo, Ruth.'

He stared at her in disgust. What the devil was he going to do with her? He crouched down on his hams in front of her till his head was a little higher than her knees and looked up into her face. He saw a face of crumpled paper in which hung two great dull eyes. Following Matron's example he picked hold of a hand, a cold bony terrible burden that he immediately wished to get rid of but did not dare. He said cajolingly, 'Remember Tommy, Ruth? Who used to play with you when you were little?'

Her habitual expression of misery did not flicker to interest or even inquiry. He tried a few more remarks uselessly and then stood up with a shrug.

'Too bad, isn't it?' said Nurse Lockwood cheerily.

'Does she hear what's said to her, do you think?'

'She can hear if she wants to, the naughty girl,' said the nurse archly.

'Well, that's something anyway. I'll come again tomorrow and maybe we could go for a little walk together and she might feel a bit more friendly. Eh, Ruth?' he shouted, bending down. 'We'll go for a little walk tomorrow you and me. Have a little chat about old times, shall us?'

The next day was Bates's lucky day; she was much brighter. She did not look at him when he came up to them, but she was no longer a stone statue of despair; she was more relaxed, more alive, she could move her head, her eyes, and arms, she could respond to exhortation.

When the nurse said, 'Come along, dear. Here's your cousin come to take you for a walk,' she obediently if mechanically stood up, waiting to be told what to do next.

'You coming with us, Nurse?'

'Well, now, do you think I'd better, or can you manage alone?'

'We're only going for a little stroll, we won't go farther than you can see. Take my arm, Ruth,' he said kindly, and off they went, Bates suiting his pace to the

216

gaunt woman's slow stumbling walk.

He chatted to her brightly, tried to rouse her attention by talking of the imaginary past when they had played together at her parents' country house. For all he knew she might not be listening, she did not even flinch when he uttered Charles's name. They ambled between shade and sun, still with her dull gaze fixed and unheeding whether he spoke of her or of himself; and the first intimation of life she gave was when a passing mad woman came muttering up and screamed something viciously into his face. Then Miss Dunville's pace quickened. Without sparing a glance for the madwoman, she almost dragged Bates away. The woman shouted after them, and turning, Bates saw her shake a fist.

'Don't listen to her,' said Miss Dunville in a slurred rusty voice, 'she's mad.'

These were the first words she had uttered in his hearing. He was so surprised that he could think of nothing to say. Into the silence between them, he heard her utter, 'You don't think I'm mad, do you?'

'No. Did anyone say you were, then?'

'There are a lot of mad people here. But I'm not mad. I don't mix with them.'

'That's right,' he said. 'It's a shame you being here with all these awful people. Don't you ever want to get away?'

She turned her head and looked at him for the first time. She was deeply astonished and a little afraid, that much he could see but he did not know why. He did not understand that this was the first time in a great while that she had had a conversation with someone outside herself. When people spoke to her she answered only her own thoughts, so that conversation ran along parallel lines that never met. This brief interchange puzzled, alarmed and excited her so much that she again lapsed into herself to consider it.

'Don't you ever want to get away from here, Ruth?' he said again.

Hardly knowing herself, she whispered, 'Yes.'

Whereupon Bates promised her that she should and proceeded to explain to her how it was to be achieved. At the end of quarter of an hour he returned her to the nurse without her having ventured another word. But although she was in her usual silent condition, the nurse's trained eye noticed the difference.

'Why, I believe you've done her good!' she said.

'I believe I have,' he agreed. 'Ruth and me are going to be friends. I'm thinking of paying her another little visit tomorrow or the next day, before I go back.' He squeezed Ruth's arm. 'You watch out for me, won't you, Ruth?'

He spent the rest of that day and all the next day making his preparations. And the day after he went to fetch Miss Dunville. She actually looked up at him when he greeted her.

'Well, Ruthie,' he said cheerily, 'you going to show me round the grounds?' He turned to the nurse, 'As it's for the last time, I thought I'd be a bit longer with her, if it won't be inconveniencing you.'

'So long as you don't make her late for her dinner. They eat at one sharp, and us poor nurses don't get fed till they're finished.'

'Oh, it would never do for Ruth to miss

her dinner, would it?' he teased. 'No, don't you worry, Nurse, I'll keep me eye on the time. You going to say goodbye to Nurse, Ruth?' But before her rusty wits could respond to this suggestion, he had seized her arm and said, 'Well, come along, then,' and marched her away.

They walked in silence for some time down the drive.

'You going to be a good girl?' he inquired. She made no reply. 'You remember what I told you?' She gave him a haunted look and pressed her hand to her head, as if the effort of memory hurt. 'Now, Ruth, there's no need to look like that: you're not mad, are you?'

She seemed to cheer up a little.

'I'm not mad,' she repeated, the faint unclear recollection of their past conversation on this theme giving her dim pleasure.

At the last turn of the drive they waited. In quite a short while Miss Dunville's face dimmed and paled with fatigue but she did not know how to express her terrible need to sit down and had to endure her exhaustion like a poor dumb beast.

They were waiting for the taxi Bates had ordered. The driver would have to hop out and ring the bell for the porter to unlock the gates for the car to pass through. The driver would tell him not to bother to shut the gates again as he would be back directly, he had come to collect a visitor, and as he was a bit on the late side the chap was sure to be waiting.

'Turn, and come back,' said Bates as the taxi drew up; the driver touched his cap with his finger and rattled on. It came back and stood panting before them like an ancient dog. Bates got Miss Dunville in. As they drew level with the lodge, Bates stuck his head out of the window to make some brief inquiry as they drove past.

'Thanks,' he nodded, as they passed through the gates and rattled on down the road.

He slid back into his own comer and slapped his hand down cheerily on the leather seat.

'Well, Ruth,' he said, 'you're out of that place for good now. How do you feel about it?'

Miss Dunville was in a shivering fit. Confusion and alarm crashed about her brain. This was too much experience all at once. It was years and years since she had been escorted on any expedition beyond the hospital grounds; twice she had been in a car in twenty years. On both occasions she had had the security of a nurse with her. She did not know who this man was, she could not remember where he was taking her or why, and she was desperately afraid, not afraid of any specific thing, just afraid of the experience itself. When he spoke she tried to listen, tried to force her mind to understand, but it was always difficult for her to concentrate and in moments of undue terror harder than ever. All her dumb soul gazed at him out of her haggard eyes.

Bates had no idea of what she was suffering and would hardly have cared if he had. His only concern was with this hazardous scheme he had to bring off. He did understand that Miss Dunville must approach the normal — in appearance, if he was to succeed, but he was a great believer in his own powers where women were concerned.

It did occur to him that she would be just the right sort of wife for him; a woman who asked no questions, never spoke, and blindly did as she was told. She would need to be his idea of a perfect wife since he must put up with her forever. The fact that, as an insane person, she could not devise a legal will, was to save her life. Since she could not will her fortune to him, he must share it with her. He had already decided that she should have a nurse and keep to her own room.

On £60,000 he could afford it, and she would be at least as comfortable as she had been in the loony bin, so he really was doing the poor wretch a good turn.

15

Lucky Mrs. Bates

The taxi drove them to Salisbury station. He had a devil of a job to get her into the train; she looked as though she thought the roaring thing was going to devour her. Luckily he got her into an empty compartment where she could collapse unremarked. She was very white and great tears kept riding her ravaged cheeks.

He said quite kindly, 'You buck up and dry your eyes, old girl; you don't want people to see you've been crying or they'll think something's up. You don't want people to think you're *mad*, do you? Back you'd have to go to that place, quick as a wink, if they thought that. You want to be careful not to act funny, Ruth. It's all right with me; you're safe with me; I know you're not mad. I'm very fond of you, Ruth, or I wouldn't have gone to all this trouble to get you out of there. Now you just remember that, when you get the wind-up; you just say to yourself, 'Tommy's looking after me.'' He gingerly patted her bony hand, and smiled encouragingly his sinister lipless grin.

When they got to London he had to buy her a nightgown and comb, she would not have thought of such a thing herself. Or having thought of it, would have been quite incapable of carrying it out. Again, he had to have a taxi to leave her in while he went into the shops; he dared not bring in this strange anguished-looking creature, nor would she have dared to enter. He just had time to nip into Woolworth's before they closed, to buy her a wedding ring to pass the landlady's eye. He had to guess the size of her finger and bought it large to be on the safe side.

'My wife has been very ill,' he told the landlady of the first respectable-looking lodging house he hit on. 'As a matter of fact,' he confided glibly, 'we've come up to see a specialist. We shall want a quiet room with two beds.' (He really could not face climbing into bed with that chilly bag of bones.) 'And my wife will need to have her meals served in her room.'

Why that most disobliging section of the human race — landladies — should have agreed to all this extra trouble is an enigma now. Perhaps she felt sorry for the poor lady. At any rate she took her up some bread-and-milk when she was in bed and a stone bottle for her feet. The poor lady said nothing, not even so much as thank you, but then her gentleman saw to all that and waited on her hand and foot, so that the landlady did not get a chance to exchange a word with the poor soul, though she was dying to hear all the gruesome details of what she hoped was a really ghastly major operation.

So far so good. But it was much too early for Bates to congratulate himself. The very next day, slipping out for a minute to buy a paper in all innocence, he received a metaphorical blow between the eyes. On the inner page there was a report about the PATIENT MISSING FROM MENTAL HOSPITAL, with full details and photo inset (a very smudged likeness, it's true, but nevertheless a rough similitude). Besides, naturally enough, there was mention of the man who was thought to have accompanied her.

The taxi-driver had mentioned that he had driven them to Salisbury station. It was thought the couple had gone to London, the report concluded guilelessly.

Bates, as the saying is, nearly died! He rushed back to their rooms and bundled their few things together. His natural agitation inspired a story for the landlady about his poor wife having to go into hospital immediately. He pressed money into her hand with gushing thanks, and the woman was so sorry for him in his distress that she even went out of her own accord to find him a taxi, a rarity in those parts.

Once again he had to face all the difficulties of transport with Miss Dunville. He hadn't even thought of where they were to go, except that he meant to put the greatest distance he could between himself and the south. At King's Cross he bundled Miss Dunville into a waiting room, but he felt all the time that people were eying her, watching him, and in his perturbation he arrived at the booking office still unprepared for the clerk's: 'Where to?' He blurted out the first name place that came into his head, goodness knows why, but perhaps it had lodged in his memory from all Frank's conversations about it.

'Two to Harrogate, single,' he said.

(Every man by his actions chooses the death he is to die.)

Once the thing was said, a multitude of ideas came pouring into his head. He knew exactly what he meant to do.

Luckily it was winter, and the north was hardly a holiday resort at that time of year. Which meant that the places that were holiday resorts in the summer would now be empty. Cottagers who took summer visitors to make both ends meet would be glad to take in someone over the winter.

As soon as they arrived in Harrogate and found suitable rooms, he got the woman to bed, locked her in the room and went out in search of a doctor.

'My wife's having a bit of a rest,' he told the landlady. 'She's not well. We've come up here for her health, and I wondered if you could recommend me a doctor.'

The woman naturally recommended

her own, which was just what he wanted. A busy man with a slum practice would not have much time to waste on querying a new patient's story. And as Bates expected, the waiting room was full of working people.

'I don't want to take up your time, doctor,' he began. And went on to explain that he was sleeping badly. He wanted some stuff a doctor had given him before that had done him a lot of good. Parallel something, he thought the name was.

'Paraldehyde?' suggested the doctor.

'That's it! It's a knockout, isn't it?'

'Two drams in a little water,' said the doctor, scribbling. 'That should do the trick. If it doesn't, double the dose. Or come back and see me again.'

'Good afternoon,' said Bates, pocketing the prescription with a cheerful smile.

The dope was to keep Miss Dunville safely asleep while he was out. He could not be away for less than several hours at a time, and he was afraid of what trouble she might get into while he was not there. He had to protect her from herself and the chance that she might try to get away, and also from the inquisitiveness of prying landladies. If she was locked in her room, asleep, he need not worry.

He was on the lookout for some small village or hamlet outside Harrogate, the sort of place which had a season for visitors.

He found a pretty little hamlet called Bathgate, some five miles away. He knocked on the door of the first cottage and asked the woman civilly if she took in lodgers.

She was a young woman, pretty in her blue overall. She looked him up and down, considering, and then said with an air of superiority, 'Naw. Ah don't.'

'Do you know anyone round here who does take in people for the summer holidays?'

'Oh, it's for the summer, is it? That's different, is that. Well, now, but you might try Mrs. Fisher as lives at Stone Croft, she does sometimes take in folk.'

'Mrs. Fisher?' he asked winningly of the old woman who opened the door of Stone Croft. He lifted his hat, and repeated his formula.

'I was recommended to you by some-one who stayed with you some years ago and said it was the happiest holiday she'd ever had,' was his line this time.

She wrapped up her arms in her apron, while she thought. Her sailor-blue eyes gazed down the years.

'Would that be Mrs. Smith?' she said at last.

'That's right. Mrs. Smith. Ever so kind to her, she said you were. And it's someone kind I'm looking for to take care of my poor wife. She's an invalid.'

'Eh, I dawn't knaw,' she said dubiously. 'It would mean a lot of work, I dare say. It's not that I wouldn't *like* to oblige, it's just that I'm getting on a bit mysel'.' Still, she asked him into the parlor, because one couldn't afford in these times to turn down good brass.

'She's no trouble,' he assured her. 'I look after her myself as a rule. But the fact is, Mrs. Fisher, we've come up here for her health. We've sold up our home and now I've got to find another. She's not fit for hotel life. So what is to become of her while I'm house-hunting? Of course I'd be coming out to see her every day; you wouldn't have to worry about that. She'll stay in her room all day and won't want more than little bits of things to eat, eggs and milk,' he suggested vaguely. 'She don't eat much, being so delikit.'

'Would it be for long,' she said, smoothing out her apron, not looking at him.

'Two or three weeks. Not more.'

'Ah'll 'ave a go,' she said.

'I knew you would,' he said. 'I knew Mrs. Smith wouldn't have given me your name if you hadn't been reliable. Now as to terms.'

They proceeded to haggle crisply for the next ten minutes, but finally came to terms: that most triumphant of bargains, where each party feels it has done down the other.

That effectively disposed of Miss Dunville for the time being and halved the danger of her being recognized. He went out to see her every day, as promised.

Sometimes she was silently crying when he arrived, and that always a little unnerved him with the dread that she might start weeping at the registry office. That would hardly do for a bride.

If she was up to the mark and the day was not too raw (he did not want her to get ill!) he would take her for a short walk, somewhere out of earshot and there try to pump into her the fact that they were going to be married and the details of the ceremony, so as to fix them in her memory.

'Now, understand, Ruth, I'm going to marry you because that's the only way for you to be safe. Then they can't get you back because you'll have a *husband* to look after you. Do you want to go back there? No, of course you don't. Then you've got to be a good girl and do what I tell you. If you don't do what I say, I'll send you back to all those mad people. I'll tell everyone you're mad.'

'I'm not mad,' she said.

'No, you're not mad; I'll say you're not! You just show me how smart you can be. Now then, listen, Ruth! 'Ruth Elinor Dunville, will you take Thomas Bates to be your lawful husband?' Go on, Ruth! What do you say? 'Ruth Elinor Dunville, will you take Thomas Bates to be your lawful husband?' . . . Go on, Ruth!'

Oh, Thomas Bates was earning his

money all right in toil and exasperated tears, sweating with nerves, and blood from the self-inflicted little wounds of his nails in the palms of his hands. The last of Annie Grun's jewelry was sold to pay these expenses. He was in terror lest he should not have enough money to pay the necessaries. The lesson went on day after day; and after fifteen days' residence in Harrogate he applied for a marriage license. Two days later he married her in his own name (this time it *had* to be legal), and took her back with him to his lodgings. Now that she was safely Mrs. Bates there was no longer any point in wasting money on two separate lodgings. One room would do for them both and he could keep her under his eye.

At once he settled down happily to draft one of his imperishable letters to the solicitors for the Dunville estate.

Sir [he wrote],
I have the honor to inform you that Miss Ruth Dunville has done me the honor to become my wife. We are resid-ing at Harrogate at present, it having

been advised as suited to her health by the doctors who are attending her. I have every hope from what they say that my wife will quite regain her best health etc., and can send you medical certificates to this effect if desired. Meanwhile, the best of care which I am naturally anxious she should have everything of the best and nurses day and night, are running me into expenses beyond my pocket and I should be obliged if you could advance a loan on the estate pending any legal arrangements necessary. Two hundred pounds would see us through current embarrassments, as specialists for instance always require being paid on the nail and this can be very awkward and has made us financially embarrassed. Please make Money Order payable through any Post Office as it will be more convenient.

Yours obediently,
Thomas Bates

How odd it was to sign his own name! He was pleased with this effort; it had to his ears the authentic authoritative ring he so much admired.

Next he drafted a letter for Ruth to copy. But he could not get her to follow it. After a few words the pen would roll across the paper, she would press her hand to her brow anxiously and tears would spring to her eyes. She could not concentrate on such a task. In any case, her writing, spindly and uncertain, gave her away with every quavering stroke. It was so long since she had written anything that she was practically incapable of forming the letters. He must think of some other way.

It was only a short letter, and after some thought and a little trouble he found a typist, through a shop-window advertisement, and got her to type it for a few pence. All Mrs. Bates would have to do now was sign it, and that should not be beyond her efforts.

The letter she was to sign, read:

Dear Sir,

I am happy to tell you that I have married Mr. Thomas Bates and am very happy. As my health is still not very good and I have bad turns quite often, I want you to make my dear husband the Power of Attorney, so that he can see to all my business for me that it is being properly run and I shall not have to worry. Please do this at once.

Bates penciled in her signature for her to go over, and she shakily inked RUTH BATES.

'All, Mrs. Bates, Mrs. Bates,' he chuckled, rubbing his hands; 'we're in the money! What a clever husband you've got, lucky Mrs. Bates!'

But not so clever perhaps. Five days later he received from the solicitors, not the money order he was expecting, but a letter to say that Mr. Jordans was coming up personally to Harrogate to wait on Mrs. Bates for her signature to the Power of Attorney.

Bates was rattled. Bates was very badly rattled. He looked uncommonly villainous as he stood there munching his fingers, desperate to find a way out.

The lawyer's letter was dated the 4th; it

was now the 6th; and Jordans was coming on the 7th. Twenty-four hours to act. Twenty-four hours in which to think of a plan and act on it. Would it be any use sending a wire to say Mrs. Bates was ill and not to come? But that would only be a postponement, and the lawyer was obviously suspicious and did not mean to part with a brass farthing until he was positive that all was as it should be. Nor would running away help; because evasion would never help to get him the money, and what Bates needed now was cash. Therefore, Jordans must be convinced; he must see Mrs. Bates, nee Ruth Dunville, see for himself that she was mentally fit to understand that she was signing her money into someone else's hands.

He would have to shake some sense into Ruth, God knows how! She must be made to understand the importance of this visit and learn the right answers to make. She must somehow appear intelligent and reasonably lively. He wondered what effect alcohol would have on her. Ready to try anything in his desperate predicament, he took the tooth glass across to *The Swan* and had a double whisky put in it.

But then he came up against her sullen obstinacy; she clenched her teeth and would not swallow. It ran out of the comers of her mouth and down her dress. He was so furious — all that money wasted! — he gave her a good slap before he could stop himself.

She stared at him, tears brightening her eyes; her white cheek reddened by the blow. It seemed to have bucked her up a bit anyway, in looks if nothing else.

It gave him an idea. She would look better with a bit of color on her face. Probably too, this man would not realize she was made up and would simply think she looked well.

But before he bothered about that he must try to make Ruth understand that she absolutely must make an effort to buck up. A gentleman was coming to see her; he would probably give her several documents to read, or would read them to her; she must say that she understood. All she need say, and keep saying, was 'Yes, I understand. I want my husband to see to everything for me.'

'That's me, Ruth. You want me to see to everything for you, don't you? You trust me, don't you? Look what I done for you! Didn't I get you away from that place where all those mad women were? Well, now, Ruth, this gentleman will make you go back there if you don't obey me. And I shan't be able to help you this time. They'll strap you up and tie your hands behind you so you're helpless, and then they'll take you away in a car without any windows. And mind you, Ruth, it won't be like it was before. They'll punish you this time for running away. And you know how they punish mad people, don't you? I dare say you've heard them screaming in that place. That's what they'll do to you. They'll put tubes up your nose to feed you. They'll put you in a strait jacket and beat you. I'm warning you, Ruth,' he said imperatively, gripping her hard by the arms and forcing her terrified eyes to meet his. 'That's what'll happen if you don't do just what I say when this gentleman comes. Jordans, his name is. You must call him Mr. Jordans. Listen to what he says and nod your head. And when he gives you a paper and tells you to write your name, what name will you put?' She stared dumbly. 'What name will you put . . . ? What is your new name . . . ? Didn't I marry you and make you Mrs . . . what? Come on, Ruth. Mrs. what?'

'Mrs. What,' she whispered dully, her eyes dim with fright.

'Mrs. *Bates*, you fool! Mrs. *Bates*! Mrs. *Bates*! Get that into your head, if you can, you blithering lunatic!' he raged. If she didn't even remember that much, however was he to cram all those other facts into her unstable head before the next day?

With nerve-wracked patience, he recommenced; warning her that if she could not even remember her own name there would not be any hope of her remaining with him, sure as eggs were eggs she would be taken back to the loony bin, shut away, never seen again. Her name was Mrs. Bates, she had been married just a week, she was very happy with her husband, and she wanted him to look after her affairs for her.

Over and over again he repeated it. At

the end of two hours, sweat pouring down his face, tears down hers, she managed to say it after him.

'There's a good girl,' he said, patting her kindly. 'Now let's have it once more. Who are you?'

She flung up her arms.

'I can't! I can't! I can't!'

'Stop that row!' he hissed, clapping his hand over her mouth. 'Do you want everyone in the house to hear? Do you want them to complain about the madwoman in number two?' She collapsed in his arms, her body jerking extravagantly to her wild sobs. He gave her a small dose of paraldehyde and let her rest for an hour. Then he began again. He had no mercy on himself, so why should he have mercy on her? There was too much at stake for him to take risks.

Before the shops shut he slipped out and bought a small box of powder, rouge and a cheap lipstick. Now he felt all was ready for the morrow and he could do no more. If ever a man had earned success he had, but he was not sanguine.

Perhaps it would have been better to let

her alone the next day and not unnerve her with so much repetition, but he never could leave well alone because he was not a person who could trust anyone or anything but himself.

So early the next morning he started going over it with her again. For five hours he pounded it into her relentlessly, alternating the recitative with arias of bullying when she faulted in her lines.

He was thankful after that he had had the thought to get some make-up for her, she looked so dreadfully haggard and white. It would not have done at all to let her be seen like that; it might make people think marriage did not agree with her.

She sat slumped in her chair, staring at the ground with her mouth open, just like the time he had first seen her on that bench in the asylum grounds.

He tipped up her heavy unresisting head and began to dab rouge on the cheekbones. He reminded her severely of that time when they thought she was so mad that she could not be trusted alone for fear of what she might do and had always to have a nurse with her.

'We don't want that to happen again, do we?' he said, as sharply suave as summer fruit. 'You must buck up, Ruth!'

She looked at him dully, unprotestingly, above the clownish red daubs on her cheeks. It was not easy, he found, to paste the lipstick evenly on her flaccid lips. By the time he had finished it looked rather a sticky mess even to his eyes. But it certainly brightened up her appearance.

16

It Was an Accident

When the landlady came up to tell him there was a gentleman downstairs asking for him, Bates said he would be down to have a word with him directly. He was particularly anxious to have a few words with this Jordans beforehand; it would give him a chance to sum him up and decide how much he could make him swallow where Ruth was concerned.

As soon as the landlady had creaked beyond earshot, he said to Ruth, 'Five minutes I'll give you, Ruth, to go over your lines to yourself, and then I'll bring him up. After that it's up to you: if he thinks you're fit to be out, it's okay; but if you forget what you have to do, he'll say you're mad, and you'll have to be put away, Ruth Bates.' (Every man by his actions chooses the death he is to die.) The door closed.

It is unimaginative people who are cruel. Bates did not mean to frighten Ruth, he only wanted to make her 'sit up a bit' and that seemed to him the best way to impress her.

In fact, it was terror that numbed her limbs and dulled her haunted mind. It was not that she really feared to go back to Lywood Asylum; however unhappy she was there in her melancholia at least it was home to her and she felt safe there, but the terrible strain of the last few weeks had filled her with unreasoning dread of any fresh experience. So much had been brought to bear on her powers of endurance that she had no reserve left, she was living in great anguish on the bare framework of her nerves. She had become so abnormally sensitive, her nerves were so exposed, so raw, that her husband's slightest movement made her jump; she flinched at a word. His threats made her feel quite on the edge of despair, a kind of rocketing vertigo, as if she had come to the verge of an abyss down which she longed to throw herself but dreaded to fall.

There was hardly room to breathe between her deafening heartbeats. On instinct she locked the door. She felt helpless, a prisoner in her own body. She could not bear it another instant. Life was a burden she could no longer carry. She flung up the window sash and with difficulty knelt trembling on the narrow sill, before she looked down . . .

She stifled a frantic impulse to scream. She fell back into the room, her legs shaking beneath her. Her huge desperate eyes gazed imploringly round the room for some way of escape. The limp bony hands moved like a blind person's across the dressing table, leaving drawers opened and empty, and groped along the mantelpiece. Her fingers closed on a cold, small, flat piece of metal. She brought it up to her eyes, darkened with the confusion of her mind. It was a penknife with which Bates had been paring his nails after breakfast. He must have put it down for a moment and forgotten it. The smallest blade was still open.

She tried horribly to moisten her dry lips. The pounding in her ears she mistook for steps on the stair, and she drew the knife sharply across her wrist. The rubbery flesh resisted the little blunt blade. Now she *could* hear steps, the sound was quite different . . .

She began to run . . . anywhere . . . nowhere . . . the little knife still open in her hand. Her blundering feet caught in the fire flex, dragging out the plug as she tripped and fell to her knees just by the empty socket.

The door handle rattled as Bates tried to turn it. She had come to the end of time. She cast one terrified look behind her to where her persecutors threatened and then twisting about, staring at the socket before her, some half-remembered impulse made her, with a kind of instinct, thrust the knife blade into the socket . . .

'Ruth!' called Bates sharply. 'Ruth! Let me in!'

They listened to the silence. Bates turned his head and met Jordans' gaze on him; they exchanged glances.

Bates bent toward the keyhole and said coaxingly: 'Ruthie, dear, it's me. Do let me in, Mr. Jordans is with me, and you don't want to keep him waiting, do you? . . . Ruthie, can you hear me?'

But there was no reply.

Bates dared not show his temper before the solicitor, but he was surging with fury that Ruth should choose this inopportune moment to play him up. He murmured sickly some excuse, which Jordans smoothly accepted, glossed over, added to, and suggested they go downstairs for another five minutes till Mrs. Bates had finished her toilet.

Jordans sat stiffly in the parlor which was cold and smelled of dust. Shadows of people outside moved across the dingy lace curtains. Bates kicked on the electric fire with the imitation flames flickering over the imitation coals. He touched the everlasting flowers in their mauve pottery vase with a housewifely gesture, nervous under Jordans' eye and this uneasy waiting which was mistimed after his careful priming.

He said at last, 'I don't suppose you ever saw Miss Dunville — Mrs. Bates, that is to say?'

Jordans looked at him critically in

silence without answering. He might have been unseeing, lost in thought. Then, as if breaking into the middle of a different and unheard conversation between them, he said, 'But since we are alone again I should like you to tell me how you came to meet Miss Dunville.'

'I thought I'd explained all that already. I come over from Australia. I'm a sort of cousin of Ruth's, and knowing no one in the Old Country, I naturally wanted to get in touch with the family. So I had private detectives to look for them for me, and what they found was Ruth. As I told you, I was sorry for the poor girl. She didn't seem to me any madder than you are. It struck me she was just neglected, being overlooked by her family and left there to molder. I didn't like the idea of that at all. It didn't seem to me right; she and me being the last of the family, as it turns out.'

'Mrs. Bates only had three aunts and I cannot trace that any of them went to Australia. You did say it was your mother was a Miss Dunville?'

'You must have misunderstood or my

tongue slipped,' said Bates quickly. 'It was my grandmother. I forget her name, if I ever knew it, she having died when I was quite a kiddy.'

Mr. Jordans' eyes were blank. 'You doubtless have documents referring to your antecedents which will quickly elucidate the point.'

'It's none of your business, that I can see, whether I got any papers or not.'

'Merely in my capacity as Miss Dunville's adviser. Of course it does not affect the immediate issue.'

'I don't see what it's got to do with any issue; I'm not in the line to inherit any of the money and I've never pretended I was.'

'No, indeed; that would be hard to prove without documentation!' exclaimed Jordans ironically. 'But of course you knew Miss Dunville was sole legatee before you asked her to come away with you.' It was more of a statement than a question.

Bates brought his coarse fingers up to his mouth. His dark glance flicked in the lawyer's direction once.

'Getting a bit close to slander, aren't

you? You'd think a lawyer would be more careful what he said. Is it likely I'd answer a question like that? I would be a fool.'

'It really doesn't require an answer, as you ably pointed out,' said Jordans, with his nearest approach to a smile shading the edge of his lips.

Bates said stiffly, 'I think we'd best be getting back. My wife will be ready now.'

But she wasn't.

Bates was appalled at this piece of underhand treachery. He did not consider that it might be something worse than that. He imagined that Ruth, warped and sullen, had taken it into her head to play this trick on him. And he could not think how to deal with it. He could not keep the man waiting. He could not threaten her in front of the man, and God knows he did not want to make a scene.

It was Jordans who came to the rescue by suggesting that she might have been taken ill, might have fainted. And Bates, with a cold feeling in his bowels, said, 'Ought we to break down the door?' It was the recollection of having been through all this — twice before — which made his hands so cold.

Jordans made him fetch the landlady, in case she had a pass key to open the door with, and in any case it was not very wise to start breaking up someone's home without explaining why first of all.

So there were three of them there when the door gave in, to stare into the empty bedroom. It was Bates who quickly stepped in and saw her lying on the floor beyond the beds. Even before he saw her arm outstretched to the plug, he could tell by her face, with its clownish make-up, what had happened. He knew that look . . . Nausea swayed up his body . . . It was like struggling through suffocating veils . . . A terrible nightmare!

He stood there like a stuck pig, staring; and it was Jordans who sent the landlady for a doctor. Jordans naturally had to ask Bates which doctor was attending his wife, and Bates dully said she had not needed one since they'd been there. It was no wonder he could not think what he was saying, he was in terror that all was lost now.

Jordans filed the reply away in his

brain; and later asked him how it was that he had not had a doctor for his wife when she was such a sick-minded person. Bates, staring at his hands, turning his wrists in their grimy cuffs, answered, 'Ruth had a horror of doctors. I couldn't ever get her to see one. Besides, I was keen for her to forget all that bad past and start a new life.'

'You realized the risk you were running? You knew she had suicidal inclinations?'

Bates turned toward him with a ghastly look. 'It was an accident. Don't you try and make out she killed herself,' he said, with an ugly expression.

'That is for the Coroner's Jury to decide,' said Jordans primly. 'But they will certainly want to know why she was not under a doctor, with her past record of ill-health.'

'Will that make it bad for me?' said Bates with grotesque naïveté.

'My dear sir,' protested the lawyer wryly.

Bates ruminated and finally said, 'My idea is, Ruth wanted to plug in the fire

— I can swear it wasn't alight when I left the room — so she goes to plug in the fire, thinking to warm the place up a bit for you, and she can't get the plug to go in. It is a bit tricky at times, but she wouldn't know that, never having had occasion to do it before. Well, then, when she couldn't get it in, she maybe had the idea there was a bit of fluff or dirt blocking up one of the holes in the socket. A woman naturally wouldn't think, she'd just pick up the first thing that came to hand to poke it out with, never giving a thought to what the article was made of. For all women know about electricity! Ruth took up this knife of mine I'd left lying around, tried to poke it in the hole, and bingo! She'd had it!' He had reason to smirk at the quickness of his brain in working out this story — after the shock he'd had too! A pretty plausible tale, he thought.

A plausible enough tale so far as it went, thought the silent lawyer, but it did not include an explanation of the locked door, for example. He made no comment, however.

Bates fidgeted in the silence while they

waited for the doctor to arrive, gnawed his stumpy fingers, and at last said crudely, 'What I'm pondering is what happens to the money if the verdict's suicide? Does suicide alter who gets it?'

17

I know the Law

Ruth died on the Friday; the inquest was held on the following Monday. A full report of it was given in the *Harrogate Herald*, published every Thursday. Frank's subscribed issue of the *Harrogate Herald* arrived in Selsey usually by the first post Saturday. He liked that because it gave him the whole week end to absorb it. He'd dip into it at breakfast Sunday and read pieces aloud to Doris, and again in the evening, if there was nothing they wanted to listen to on the radio, he would select gossipy bits to tell her. She never bothered to read it herself.

The report of the inquest was on page 3, sandwiched between BUS COLLISION, FIVE INJURED and FARMHOUSE ROOF BLOWN OFF IN 70 M.P.H. GALE. But Frank's eye was caught first by the center headlines: ELECTROCUTED BRIDE INQUEST.

Those words would always draw his attention now; a macabre souvenir of poor Grace. As he read he felt the skin of his face grow cold and taut.

The week-old bride of Thomas Bates, engineer, who tragically met her death last Friday from an electric shock, was identified at the inquest in Coroner's Hall on Monday as a patient who escaped from Lywood Asylum a month ago suffering from neurasthenia.

Mrs. Tipcross, householder, of 12 Borough St., where the couple resided, described how Mr. Bates and a companion broke open the bedroom door in her presence and discovered the deceased on the floor, holding a steel penknife, the blade of which was inserted in one of the apertures of an electric-power wall plug.

Mrs. Tipcross testified that when she went to tell Mr. Bates of his visitor, she heard him talking to his wife. In about two minutes he followed her downstairs, and she heard the two men mount to the first floor as the clock struck the quarter. About half past four they called to her to ask if she had a pass key as they could not get an answer from Mrs. Bates and they feared she had been taken ill. They then proceeded to break in the door.

The deceased had been with her a week, and Mr. Bates, who came there a fortnight previous, had told her his wife was in a nursing home and he visited her there every day. When he brought her home, Mrs. Tipcross saw that the lady was an invalid she had all her meals in her room and her husband waited on her hand and foot. Mrs. Tipcross saw her when she brought up the meals, but she never spoke, and Mrs. Tipcross concluded that her illness was some affliction of the larynx.

Dr. Wilshire of Lywood Asylum formally identified the dead woman as his patient and described her malady as chronic melancholia, from which she had suffered for a number of years. He described the characteristic symptoms as extreme depression, together with marked disinclination for speech, and almost total inactivity of any kind. Melancholics needed constant attention, very often requiring to be hand fed. They usually lacked the impulse to self-preservation and were liable to strong suicidal compulsions.

A juryman asked whether a sudden change of scene and circumstance, as in this instance getting married and removing to another part of the country, might not prove sufficiently beneficial to effect a temporary cure?

Dr. Wilshire replied that while such a contingency was not outside the bounds of possibility, he was strongly of the opinion that it was not very probable. He considered it more likely that undue strain on an unbalanced mind had precipitated a crisis.

Dr. Wilshire added in conclusion that the marriage had not been consummated.

There was some rather incomprehensible testimony from the dead woman's solicitor, who had apparently been one of the people to discover the body. He had come from London to see his client on business, but death had intervened before he saw her. Although he had acted for her professionally on one or two occasions, he had never met her and could not identify her. He nevertheless had every reason to believe that the woman was who she was supposed to be.

There was also the testimony of the local police surgeon and the police. Brief and very technical, but it gave Frank a clear enough outline of what had happened, of the woman half-kneeling, half-lying on the ground, her arm rigidly outstretched.

Then it went on:

The deceased's husband (photo back page) vigorously denied that his wife had shown any suicidal leanings since he had known her. He admitted that he had helped and encouraged her to escape from the mental hospital. He had gone there to see her and she had appealed to him to get her away. The only way he knew of to make her safe was by marrying her, and he did this solely to safeguard her. He had never believed that she was as mentally sick as the doctors made out. She always seemed quite normal with him, though he noticed she was shy with strangers. He firmly believed that if she was happy she could get quite well.

His reason for not having a doctor to attend her was because her experiences had made her deeply suspicious of them and he was most reluctant to rouse in her unhappy memories unnecessarily.

He would like the opportunity to explain how it came about that the window was open though the day was so cold. Earlier in the afternoon his wife had complained of faintness and asked him to turn off the electric fire, with which request he had complied and opened the window for her too.

Later, after he had left the room, he surmised she must have wished to turn on the fire for the benefit of their visitor but had been unable to force the plug home. It was inclined to be awkward to insert. He fancied that she must have thought some dirt was blocking the holes in the socket so that the pins could not slide in, and attempted to clear them, unthinkingly using the blade of his knife for the purpose.

He had been speaking to her within a few minutes of her death and nothing that was said led him to suppose the idea of suicide was in her mind.

The jury returned a verdict of 'Death by Misadventure' and asked if they might express their sympathy with the bereaved husband.

Dr. Horton, the Coroner, declined to pass on the message of sympathy and expressed his disapproval of the widower's actions by rebuking him for having removed the lady from the place where she was receiving every care and attention, reprimanding him for culpable negligence in not at least putting her in the care of a qualified mental doctor.

The bereaved husband left the court in tears.

But the photograph on the back page was smiling. The head was turned a little away from the camera; but that delicate bony jaw, the hollowed eyes, the wide grin of that lipless mouth, surely, surely, there was no mistaking them?

Old Frank's heart thumped. He felt as if a rope was round his neck, choking him, and he ran a finger inside his collar.

He went to the door and called. When Doris came he showed her just the photo on the back page of the folded newspaper.

'Who does that remind you of?'

She studied it. He held it away from her floury hands, keeping his own thumb carefully over the description.

'I don't know,' she said at last. 'Who?'

'You mean to say you don't *know*?' he cried incredulously, quivering with excitement and vexation.

'It doesn't look like anyone to me,' she said indifferently, annoyed with the maddening ways of husbands who calmly called you to leave your cooking, as if it was a matter of life and death, and then it was merely to show you a photograph of someone who looked like someone else.

'Oh, my lord, don't I always say you

women are the most unobservant crea-
tures on God's earth! What's the good of
being able to describe Mrs. Jones's new
hat or the gussets in the back of her coat,
when you don't recognize the speaking
image of a man you lived next door to for
months!'

'Gussets in the back of a coat! Really,
Frank, you are a silly old man,' Doris said
good-humoredly, and went back to her
kitchen.

Frank followed her. 'No, I wish you'd
be serious, Doll, this is important. Have
another look.'

She squinted at it obligingly. 'Yes, it
does look like someone, but I can't think
who.'

'What about Freddy Noble — as he
called himself?'

She stared at the picture again, and
said conciliatingly, 'Yes, it is vaguely like,
I suppose. He was dark, I expect that
makes a difference. This man is fair.'

'It's only the way the light falls on his
hair makes it look like that. Can't you see
that's just the way he used to smile?'

'It's not unlike,' she agreed peaceably.

'Pass me that cup, dear.'

Frank realized that he should have started the story from the other end. Then she would have been struck by the likeness. He proceeded to unfold it.

'So you think it's poor Grace's husband, do you?' she said, not looking at him but at the pastry board she was sprinkling with flour.

Frank looked at her coldly. He better understood how her mind worked than she knew. Big, white-skinned, red-haired, dominating, she could run rings round him nine times out of ten because he was obsessed by her and honestly thought she was too exalted and brilliant to be tied to such an old fogy as he was. Still, there are times when a man is always right. This was one of them.

'Prove to me they're the same person,' she said.

'The whole set-out from beginning to end is the same: the man leaving his wife while she is still alive to give himself an alibi, then the locked door and fetching witnesses to watch him break it in and find the dead body. I don't know how much more you want unless it's a signed confession.'

She held her hands under the tap, as if she were washing them of the whole affair. 'Well? What are you going to do about it?' she said.

But after her obstructionism Frank was no longer in the mood to discuss the matter with her, and recollecting a prewar pamphlet that had puzzled him with its title, he said loftily, 'I am not going to do nothing,' and left it at that.

He went to the police. The solitary constable told him the superintendent was out.

'When do you expect him back?'

'Couldn't say, sir. Can I help?'

'It's important,' he hesitated. 'The sergeant would do.'

The policeman went next door.

'There's an old woman wants to see the Super, about something very important, he says; but you'll do. Will you see him?'

'Find out what it's about.'

With an expressionless face the constable reported back that it was about a death by misadventure that had taken place in Harrogate the previous week which the gentleman wished to connect with the accidental death of Mrs. Noble of Beach Edge last summer.

'Oh, a crank!' moaned the sergeant. 'I suppose I shall have to see him. Show him in.'

He listened with an air of dull patience to Frank's tale but his restless pencil-tapping fingers betrayed him. Halfway through his story Frank sensed his disbelief and from then his narrative sagged and flagged. Although the sergeant promised to look into it, he knew that nothing would be done and even suspected a smile beneath the constable's mustache, which made him flush with anger. He did not care to be laughed at. It was a triumph for Doris. So that night he put the cutting in an envelope and scribbled a note to accompany it.

Dear Pickering,

I think you ought to see this. I should explain that I took it upon myself to show it to the local police (as there seemed no time to lose if the man is not to escape again) but they were not interested.

The cutting was like a thunderbolt in his hand to Pickering. The last few months had been spent in trying to find the man who had bigamously married his daughter and perhaps murdered her too. Pickering tried to preserve an open mind about that, simply because he had always prided himself on being a broad-minded man who did not jump to conclusions. But despite his determined open-mindedness, he had become a man with a mania. If the police called Doris' husband an old woman and a crank, Pickering they called a fanatic.

This new piece of information he took straight to Scotland Yard, where he saw the inspector he had seen before. Now the inspector had reason to be very interested in Pickering's narration. A City firm of solicitors represented by a man named Jordans had already been in touch with him, asking for information about a certain type, who it turned out was the man in the news cutting, called Thomas Bates. If Thomas Bates was the same person as Pickering's bigamous son-in-law then the inspector would have some interesting news for Mr. Jordans. Meanwhile he advised Mr. Jordans to lie low and say nothing.

Thomas Bates was once again going through one of his heart breaking struggles with a lawyer. He could not get Jordans to commit himself to saying whether he inherited the money or not. It had got to the point where Jordans refused to see him — Bates was back in London now — or answer his bombardment of letters. So Bates got himself a lawyer of his own to protect his interests — a Greek shyster.

Padiapolous, the little Greek, had no doubt whatsoever that his client was legally entitled to his wife's fortune. He was so sure that he was on to a good thing that he went so far as to introduce his client to a gentleman who would advance him some cash. Now, where money was concerned Padiapolous had the slippery fingers of a conjurer, and those crisp notes would never have found their way into Bates's pocket if the Greek had not been certain he would get it back three times over. Besides, Bates was absolutely on the rocks, stony broke, down-at-heel, desperate again, and seething with bad temper. If something wasn't done to help him, the Greek would lose his client altogether.

Padiapolous said grandly, 'We shall bring suit against this unscrupulous firm for fraud.'

This was a man after Bates's own heart; unafraid, threatening, making the Law a mere instrument of twisted meanings with which to pick the lock of Justice.

Thus, a few days later Padiapolous announced with pride, implying it was all due to his cleverness, that Jordans had agreed to see Bates and had made an appointment for the following afternoon.

'I go with you,' said Padiapolous, 'to watch your interests.'

And that was how it came about that when the two men, almost invisible in their dark coats in the dark corner of Fenchurch St. Buildings, came between Bates and his companion, crowding against Bates to say, 'Are you Thomas Bates? I have here a warrant for your arrest for the murder of Ruth Dunville,' the little Greek was there to cry out excitedly, waving his hands, 'Don't say anything, sir! Keep your mouth shut!' even before the detective had time to utter the official warning.

Bates laughed.

He was not strongly represented with that risible instinct which we call 'a sense of humor,' but that struck him as shatteringly funny. He would have liked to explain to the little Greek just how funny it was. The British detective was the biggest bloody fool in the world!

Then he suddenly became quite sober, not to say severe, and warned them that they were making a terrible mistake.

Padiapolous danced around, wringing his hands. 'For Christ's sake, sir, don't say *anything!*'

'That's okay, Perdappullus. They won't think it so funny when I sue them for unlawful detention.' He gave his crooked smile. 'I know the law,' he said.

18

Take Away This Heart of Stone

As a relief from the fuel crisis, the alleged murder of Ruth Dunville was accorded quite a lot of publicity in the daily press. Bates was charged at Bow Street and remanded. The public prints of the alleged murderer brought four different people to present themselves at Scotland Yard with fresh information about his past.

There was Clara Bead, a servant girl he had 'married' before the war. Strangely enough she was not concerned with him as a murderer at all, she simply wanted to take him back. She had come to claim him as her proper husband. When she saw Bates at the identification parade she burst into tears.

'That's Charlie. How he's changed!' she wept.

How different from Annie Grun, all

venom. She had been looking for him through the police for months, determined ostensibly to get back her jewelry. But there was something more than that goading her on too, so that as she lay sleepless through half the night she gratified the injury to her pride and self-esteem by devising slow impossible torments for him. She lay taut in the dark, her heart banging painfully against her side from these imaginings. At the identification parade she hurried past him with barely a glance, only her face reddened darkly.

It was the fact that she had married a thief that she couldn't get over. 'You got to get back all my jewelry,' she told the Yard, and described it passionately piece by piece. 'Left me without a cent, he did, the dirty little rotter, after only two days.' All he'd left her with was her marriage lines — for what they were worth! — and a handkerchief he'd forgotten that didn't even belong to him. She'd brought it with her, with her marriage lines, in case they wanted to see them. It was fine linen marked with a name tape that read

Dennis Titmuss. Most likely he'd stolen that too, the rotten little thief. It might have been returned by mistake by the laundry, but she didn't think so; having been in the cleaning trade all her life she knew about laundry marks and this one was different from his, not the same firm even.

Scotland Yard was very interested in that handkerchief by the time the grocer's deposition came into their hands. So Morris Fennel became the third witness of the identification parade.

Oddly enough it was Bates who turned a faded yellow when he saw the bat-eared grocer earnestly scanning the line. It sickened Bates with its sinister hints of a great net spreading . . . He could not fathom how they could have got hold of Fennel or why he was there. For the first time he felt afraid.

The fourth person did not participate in the identification parade, did not need to. A tall lean figure in vaguely clerical black; long-fingered, menacing, his great shadow stretched across from Bates's childhood, darkening the present with the sour taste of the past. He was Warden of the Institution which had sheltered Bates, which had guarded and guided his little mind and turned him into an obedient boy, suitably grateful to everyone for charity received. The Warden was the stern father whose approval must be won and who meted out punishment; he was also the mother at whose knees the four hundred and fifty little boys learned to lisp their prayers. He spoke of them as his big family. He was, in fact, no different from the head of any large school, in that some of the boys feared him, some hated him; most in the end came to revere him. Bates feared him, deeply longed for his approval, and left despising him for not having valued Bates at his true worth.

The Yard looked up the accounts of the Titmuss inquest. Electrocution again! And the fresh knowledge that the man Bates had learned his trade apprenticed to an electrician. It seemed they had got the case tied up with blue ribbons.

Bates was brought before the Magistrates and committed for trial.

It took about six weeks to prepare the

trial, involving some hundreds of people in work behind the scenes. And while all this was in progress Bates lay idle in Brixton, the still center of this cyclonic activity. Sometimes the warders passing his cell heard him laughing. This pleasant natural sound gave a singularly unpleasing and unnatural effect in those surroundings.

'He needs to have his head examined,' said one warder dryly to another.

He was examined in the course of things by the prison doctor and a couple of specialists; but he was much too sure of himself at this stage to wish to pretend insanity. So he was declared fit to plead.

Padiapolous, frightened, had thrown in his hand long before; and Bates's defense was undertaken by the firm of Trufitt and Johnson, the well-known criminal lawyers. Although their client was not a likable man, his story seemed credible enough and clear. He never wavered in his narration of events when they pressed him, seeing dangerous points that the prosecution might make much of. He was carelessly positive about his innocence, and showed not the least anxiety about the outcome.

His line was that Ruth's death had been an accident. 'The Coroner said so,' he complained indignantly, large-eyed.

It was a different affair when he learned that he was to be charged additionally in the indictment with the murders of Titmuss and Pickering. It was a long time before they could calm him down. He seemed to have the idea that the law was a kind of game in which each side tried to get the better of the other, cheating where possible.

'They can't do this!' he raved. 'They can't bring up all this old stuff against me!'

His lawyer did not find it easy to convince him that they could.

'We shall object of course; but we must know precisely where we stand and what objections we can raise.'

'I wasn't even there when they died,' declared Bates indignantly. 'A nice thing if a person is going to be accused of murdering a person every time they die accidentally.'

★   ★   ★

The trial of Rex v. Bates began on March 19, a day of gray boisterous winds, and took place in the Central Criminal Court of the Old Bailey. The accused came up into the dock and looked about him coolly. Fie had put on flesh in prison and in his dapper suit looked quite a harmless, not ill-looking little gent, hanging on the fringes of respectable dishonesty. As usual the eyes and mouth gave him away; he was not a man you would trust, but he no longer presented that appearance of livid menace oddly heightened by his air of childish frailty.

Bates listened with uncomprehending and insolent calm to his indictment for the murder of Ruth Dunville on three counts (the second and third counts respectively the murders of Dennis Titmuss and Grace Pickering).

M'Gillycuddy K. C., the great rhetorical Irish bull, was Senior Prosecutor. Bates pretended to listen with a smile to his exposition. From time to time he stabbed down some penciled words on a pad he held and then looked up and about him again with his smug air of triumph. What he scrawled down was indecipherable but it was of no significance anyway; what mattered was the act he was building up. He was under no illusion about his own importance in the issue. He was pleased to see there were a nice lot of women in the public gallery — he only wished there were more women in the jury. He turned his head from side to side, letting his eyes rest enigmatically on some woman's face till she shifted uneasily; and so from one to another, counting how many pairs of eyes were watching him rather than the *mouvementé* black gown in the center of the floor.

The job of Defending Counsel, Mr. Whyte-Whittier K. C., was not an easy one, with its ominous echoes of G. J. Smith. His client had so much against him, so much more than he seemed to realize. Whyte-Whittier's line was to emphasize the pale unstained innocence of his past (with the Warden for witness to his pathetic beginnings in the Institution) and darting wherever possible a momentary beam of light into the blameless periods of his life. Fretting his solitary way through time and with no employers to testify to his hard-working probity, nothing to account for the spent years, it had been comparatively easy for Bates to concoct a history for Whyte-Whittier to work on.

Bates sunned himself delightedly in his Counsel's tale of virtue and pathos; he listened to it as if every word of it were true. Indeed, it did in some strange way seem true to him; it was the truth of what *should* have happened. He was that noble, down-trodden, misunderstood man, and he thought all the more highly of Counsel for seeing into his true nature; he felt a flood of emotion for this great-souled man, and was surprised to feel it. He had not liked Whyte-Whittier when first they met, nor trusted him; had indeed been deadly afraid of those eyes and the horrible cutting questions that made evasion so difficult.

It was Counsel's contention that Ruth Dunville's death had been an accident and nothing but an accident — or misadventure, as the Coroner's Inquest had decided at the time.

It was the only possible line he could take, after all; but as it happened to be true, Bates found it very heartening and soothing to hear.

Unfortunately, it made the Prosecution's charge of rebuttal an easy one.

The Prosecution's answer to the defense of 'accident' was to to ask the jury if they could believe that the same *accident* could happen to one man three times?

There was the case of Dennis Titmuss found dead by electrocution (Coroner's verdict 'Death by Misadventure') in a bathroom locked on the inside; Bates, under the alias of Hardy, residing with him at the time.

There was the case of Grace Pickering found dead by electrocution (Coroner's verdict 'Death by Misadventure') in a bathroom locked on the inside; Bates, under the alias of Noble, living with her, ostensibly as her husband.

There was the case of Ruth Dunville found dead by electrocution (Coroner's verdict 'Death by Misadventure') in a room locked on the inside; Bates having been her husband for a week.

'How could I lock the doors on the inside?' screamed Bates angrily.

'You are here to answer the Court's questions; we are not here to answer yours,' was the stern reply.

'He's just saying anything that comes into his head,' Bates shouted. 'That's not proof! How could I have shut Grace in the bathroom and locked the door on the inside when I was two miles away, tell me that?'

The warder hastily pulled him down. The well of the Court was pink with faces upturned to him. They looked shocked.

'Silence..! Silence . . . Silence . . . ' went all round the Court.

Enraged (for wasn't he the most important person there? and what was the use of him being there if he had to sit mum like a wooden image while people told lies about him as they pleased?), enraged, then, he leaned forward on his folded arms to demand of the Judge if this wasn't supposed to be a Court of Justice where they were to hear the *whole* truth and nothing *but* the truth? 'Or so help me God!' he concluded sardonically.

This piece of impudence did him no good. It only made the Judge livid.

An English Criminal Court is not a place for low comedy. Its pomp and dignity crush impertinence, though what threats can intimidate a man on trial for his life, it is hard to say. However, the Judge's quiet ancient voice caused Mr. Bates to subside at once.

But only momentarily. Soon he was jumping up to expostulate again. Soon he was shrieking abuse at the witnesses against him: at Pickering, who was telling how Bates had simply espoused Grace for her Savings and run away with them. Letters were read aloud, startling in their crudity.

'That's a lie!' Bates yelled. 'I paid it back every penny at $4\frac{1}{2}$ per cent, and gave her a diamond brooch besides, which I got witnesses to prove!'

It is hard to say whether Hewbank or Jordans were the more austerely harmful to him, describing his clumsy and naive attempts to claim money from them to which he was not entitled; their accounts made him appear not only stupid but ruthless.

There were Morris Fennel and Frank to describe his curious behavior on the occasions that Titmuss and Grace Pickering met their deaths 'by Misadventure.' His strange conviction, in both instances, that the victims were dead, before they had been 'discovered.' Frank in particular had remarked that he seemed as cool as a cucumber, not the least upset, although he kept assuring Frank that he was. In fact, when he burst in on them, they had received the impression that he was about to burst out laughing, except that he flung his hands up to hide his face. His callous disregard for the corpse was of course more noticeable with his wife than with Titmuss, a comparative stranger. When Frank had reprimanded him for leaving the dead woman lying on the floor like a carcass of mutton, the accused remarked that when 'they' were dead 'they' were done for.

On the other hand there was the unshakable evidence that he had left the house after Grace Pickering (Doris and

Frank were committed to testifying that they had heard him calling to Grace out at sea that Sunday morning and that later they had seen Grace return to the house, half an hour before the accused returned) and the owner of Sam's Cafe could vouch for the time he was there.

The evidence of the metal switch covers Whyte-Whittier cleverly managed to turn in the prisoner's favor to a great extent. He made the man who had sold the prisoner the metal switch covers admit that, though the brass ones had become unfashionable, the plastic ones might break . . . the accused had brought him in a broken one to show him why he wanted to change them. Whyte-Whittier also brought in an electrical expert whose opinion it was that a man who knew just a little about electricity might well not realize how unsafe it was to put a metal cover on to a partly corroded switch, while yet being able to appreciate the danger from a broken plastic one.

Whyte-Whittier declared that what the Prosecution was pleased to regard as proof of murder amounted to no more than the dumb misery of a man too shocked to express his frozen horror at the tragedy that had befallen him for a second time (the case of Dennis Titmuss, Whyte-Whittier dismissed with a wave of the hand, since there was no motive).

But the trio of deaths was not so negligible to the jury. They could not ignore the terrible coincidences of the victim springing the death trap alone while the murderer coolly chats to a stranger who will innocently provide him with an alibi; they could hardly ignore the electrical device on which the death trap was always based, nor the trick of witnesses being brought to vouch for the door being locked before they broke in to 'discover' the body. Even the fact that this time he had legally married — or thought he had legally married — his victim told against him, since he stood to benefit by her death. That the poor creature was half mad made it all the more shocking. The tissue of lies he had woven for the occasion, beginning with his Australian cousinship, was unraveled before their eyes.

For a habitual liar there is nothing more dismaying than not to be believed when one is telling the truth. It rattled Bates, even before the ordeal of examination and cross-examination. He had been looking forward to that lime-lit moment in his anticipations; always the hero of all his own dreams. Grace could have told him, dreams go by contraries. He did not appear to advantage in the witness box.

Whyte-Whittier realized too late that he would have done better for his client not to have put him in the 'box'; but that in itself was always regarded as such a damaging admission that he had not dared not to call him in his own defense.

He turned out a shabby figure and a liar, losing his temper, growing sullen, veering from the mendicant's whine to shrill abuse.

'You tell me how I could make anyone, however potty, touch off a live wire with a bit of steel against their will?' he screamed repeatedly.

He kept demanding to be told how he could have locked the door on the inside, instead of answering the questions put to him by Counsel. It was terrible to see M'Gillycuddy corner him, bully him to the edge of hysteria or until there was no alternative but for him to say sulkily that he refused to answer that question.

M'Gillycuddy's closing speech was a well-knit argument that accounted for every curious factor in the case against Thomas Bates, recapitulating that while it might be an unfortunate accident that Bates was of the household when Dennis Titmuss met his death, it was surely a sinister coincidence that a few months later the woman he had bigamously espoused should have met her death similarly, having *just* signed a will in his favor; and to the third death, again only a few months later, again with all external similarities, again with the hope of benefiting ultimately by the death, but his immediate aim to safeguard himself from exposure — the prisoner being obliged to kill her before she could reveal the true state of affairs to her solicitor (the jury had heard how the solicitor's suspicions had been aroused by the letters he received demanding money).

Whyte-Whittier did his best. He was eloquent enough. Too eloquent perhaps, for his impassioned pleas elided several unanswerable points on the Crown's side.

The Judge's summing up was scrupulously just, delivered in a sub-acid voice. As the jury filed out, Whyte-Whittier permitted himself to shrug his shoulders and fling up his hands, as an expression of opinion.

The jury were away an hour and seventeen minutes. Bates spent the time renewing his appearance, making himself impeccable. He was not unduly optimistic, the last day had ruffled him, but he still firmly believed that he could not be accounted guilty for a crime he had never committed. He mounted cheerfully the stone steps to the dock, passed a few pleasant remarks to the warder and gazed about him with his peculiarly knowing supercilious smile.

The foreman of the jury, Bates noticed, kept his eyes nervously away from the fascination of the dock. For the first time, Bates's heart sank, his fingertips were icy against his cheek, remembering something he had heard or read, that when the jury's verdict was unfavorable they never looked at the prisoner.

But he was not long in suspense. Almost at once he heard the Clerk of the Court ask if they had arrived at a verdict, and the foreman's answer toll solemnly into the silence:

'GUILTY.'

'Is that the verdict of you all?'

'It is.'

The Clerk of the Court cried, 'Thomas Bates, you stand convicted of murder; have you anything to say why the Court should not give you judgment of death, according to law?'

Bates nodded. His tongue cleaving to the roof of his mouth made speech impossible.

'Say on,' said the Judge.

He had to use his fingers to loosen his locked tongue. Then his voice broke into a howl, 'I swear before God I am innocent! I never have done this terrible crime they have brought against me!'

In the silence that followed, Mr. Justice Lyell prepared to pass sentence.

Bates became aware that the warder

was holding him by the arm. He *wanted* his knees not to hold him up, he wanted to sink and sink and sink peacefully down into the earth, hearing no more, bearing no more. There was a sob like an agonizing pain in his chest struggling to burst out. He was in terror. Half dead with fright, he thought he was dying, straining through the horrible dimness to the Judge's face.

(The black cap was only a square of silk, nothing to fear . . .)

He listened carefully to the Judge's slow sentence because he wished not to hear him say the piece about being hanged by the neck till he was dead. When those words came Bates muttered as loud as he was able, 'The trial has been unfair!' No one ever knew what he said because it came out in an indistinct croak; but for him it had succeeded in drowning out the sickening words.

Then the Court was full of noise, and he was hustled away. There were three weeks left for Thomas Bates in which to make his soul. Instead he soothed himself with a lullaby, rocking over and over in his mind, 'I shall appeal! I shall appeal!' He still refused to believe they could hang him, because he had not killed Ruth Dunville, and it would be an intolerable injustice. He clung to that, as though Justice had always been his watchword.

The appeal failed. He stood before the Appellant Judges incredulously. It was impossible! It must be a mistake . . . a miscarriage of justice. Or a conspiracy. He became convinced it was a plot conceived by Pickering, by Hewbank and Jordans, to get him out of the way and seize the money. The two warders watched him incuriously, raving up and down his cell . . .

The petition to the Home Secretary failed.

Bates sat on his bunk in frozen disbelief.

There was a week to go . . . three days to go . . . twenty-four hours left . . . The prison chaplain regularly visited him, offering him consolation, offering him salvation, offering him the promise of God's patient mercy.

But the least suggestion that Bates was not innocent drove him storming out of his frozen silence, to shriek out his vows against Heaven that he was sinless. He was the heart of innocence in a guilt-stained world!

The prison chaplain, inured to the painful spectacle of obstinate sin, never ceased to pray for him; he prayed aloud for God in His Mercy to take away Bates's heart of stone and to give him a heart of flesh that could bleed and suffer . . .

For a long time now Bates had heard only the echo of his own terrors when people spoke to him; but he heard the chaplain's prayer and bitterly resented it. He crossed his hands on his breast and said loudly: 'Blessed is he, whosoever shall not be offended in me!' and his crooked smile was sly with pride.

★   ★   ★

The last morning they don't give you much time to brood; the machinery of death moves at a brisk military pace. The prisoner in their hands is scuffled about like a dummy. This is not brutality but distaste for what is to come. They have been through it before.

Bates suffered them with a smile of pale contempt, secure in his disbelief: they could not do this to *him*.

He was bundled ignominiously into the yard. In this ancient prison there was no execution shed and it was still the custom to erect the gallows in the prison yard. But it was not the sight of that crude black geometry against the dusty blue sky that caused his legs to fold beneath him; it was the sudden incredible uproar assaulting his flesh that burst out as he appeared. This appalling howl was carried on the clear air from the ramshackle tenements distantly overlooking the prison yard; it could even be seen that every window was crammed with red-and purple-faced figures, banging metal, calling, waving, shrieking hysterically, with hatred and with *laughter* . . .

That there should be *laughter* was shocking. The scene itself appeared to quiver with the gruesome inhuman racket. The astonishing spectacle of so much hatred all directed at him seemed completely to unnerve Bates; terror of this hydra-headed monster suddenly loosened his knee joints and turned his bowels, with its intimations of a punishment he had never foreseen; so that he had to be dragged across the yard, lifted to the scaffold, and held upright there while his last glimpse of the world was extinguished in the stuffy folds of cloth that smelt like death itself.

Instantly he dropped away.

His stony heart rolled thunderously to a stop, like a boulder shutting him into a sepulcher forever.

We do hope that you have enjoyed reading this large print book.

Did you know that all of our titles are available for purchase?

We publish a wide range of high quality large print books including:
**Romances, Mysteries, Classics
General Fiction
Non Fiction and Westerns**

Special interest titles available in large print are:
**The Little Oxford Dictionary
Music Book, Song Book
Hymn Book, Service Book**

Also available from us courtesy of Oxford University Press:
**Young Readers' Dictionary
(large print edition)
Young Readers' Thesaurus
(large print edition)**

For further information or a free brochure, please contact us at:
**Ulverscroft Large Print Books Ltd.,
The Green, Bradgate Road, Anstey,
Leicester, LE7 7FU, England.
Tel:** (00 44) **0116 236 4325
Fax:** (00 44) **0116 234 0205**

MYSTERY OF THE RUBY

V. J. Banis

According to legend, the Baghdad ruby has the power to grant anything the heart desires. But a curse lies upon it, and all who own the stone are destined to die tragically, damned for eternity. When Joseph Hanson inherits the gem after his uncle's bizarre murder, his wife Liza is afraid. Though his fortune grows, he becomes surly and brutal. And suddenly Liza knows there's only one way to stave off the curse of centuries — she must sacrifice her own soul to save the man she loves.